Spare Change

Michael Anthony Adams, Jr.

SIX SEEDS PRESS
Baltimore, MD

First Edition
Copyright © 2022 Michael Anthony Adams, Jr.

Originally published in paperback by Six Seeds Press
Baltimore, MD
July 2023

ISBN: 978-1-952240-32-4

All rights reserved.

The stories presented here are works of fiction. Names, characters, places, and incidents are the product of the author's imagination or are used fictitiously. Any resemblance to actual persons, living or dead, events or locales is entirely coincidental.

Cover Design © 2023 PJ Adams
Portrait of Michael Anthony Adams, Jr. © 2014 PJ Adams

An earlier version of *I Want to Talk to You* originally appeared on *The Charles Carter* website under the pen name Israfel Sivad on April 10, 2020. Earlier versions of *Maybe the Afterlife Is Our Real Life*, *Moonshadow*, and *Sometimes You Have to Jump the Snake* originally appeared on the blog *Pan de Bare* between October 2019 and February 2020. All other stories are previously unpublished.

Also by Michael Anthony Adams, Jr. and Published by Six Seeds Press

Novels:
The Adversary's Good News
Crossroads Blues

Short Stories:
Spare Change
Psychedelicizations
The American Apocalypse
The Cars Behind, Beside Us
Welcome to the Modern World, Charlie
Notes from the Idle Mind

Poetry:
We Are the Underground
From Now to You
Recipe for a Future Theogony
Indigo Glow
The Tree Outside My Window
At the Side of the Road

Memoir:
Disorder

www.MichaelAnthonyAdamsJr.com

Spare Change
For PJ

I Want to Talk to You	9
Do You Even Own Any Red, White, and Blue?	23
Isn't It?	37
For It Is in Giving That We Receive	45
Our Only Hell	53
Embracing the Devil at the Heart of This World	67
And I Will Make You Fishers of Spare Change	81
Johnny and Bruce Were Friends	93
We're Really Going to Do Some Damage Now	105
Sometimes You Have to Jump the Snake	115
Thank You So Much for Coming	127
Maybe the Afterlife Is Our Real Life	135
Moonshadow	143
And What Might Those Ideas Be?	159

Spare Change

I Want to Talk to You

"I want to talk to you about racism and gentrification," was the first thing the man walking down the sidewalk said to Matthew on that summer day. The younger white man had stepped out on his stoop to enjoy the sunshine, and he'd just begun reading for his required classes starting that September. Now, it was December a year and a half later. If there was anything the year before had taught a law student like Matthew about December, it was one thing: stress. From exams and Christmas. His exams were taken care of for the moment. Matthew had left the Georgetown Law Library about 15 minutes earlier. He'd been sitting there since early that morning, trying to concentrate on the intricacies of Constitutional Law. Now, it was evening. Outside, the sky had already turned a dusky gray, but Matthew was inside walking through a crowd in the Metro station at Gallery Place, waiting for a green line train to take him back up to Columbia Heights. He wanted to pick up some cards for his family that night, and he figured the Target in his neighborhood might be a good place to start. Living off loans, he'd really stretched himself thin the year before when he'd tried to get presents for his parents and younger sisters. He didn't want to do that again. Besides, this year he had a girlfriend.

As he descended an escalator to the station's lowest level, his mind swam with contradictions about how one could interpret the foundations of the United States' government. No god had delivered those rules inviolable throughout millennia. No tablets carried them writ in stone immutable through all the centuries. Laws depended upon human experience to create them. They needed human minds to understand them. They required human beings to enforce them. It was something Matthew had always known, but it wasn't something always so translucently clear. Suddenly, the significance of his ability to form his own interpretations of the massive case law books in his backpack struck him with the force of a Metro train. The implications had never been so apparent. He would be one of an elite group of citizens responsible for the curation of those concepts passed down from generation to generation for more than two hundred years. He would argue ideas predicated upon how the past had understood those regulations for governing such a massive body politic as the United States of America. He would assist in determining how the future might elucidate those collections of complex sentences that could give or take life, liberty, and the pursuit of happiness from any man or woman.

With such lofty thoughts swirling through his brain, Matthew reached the bottom of the escalator. He wasn't paying much attention to the world beyond his own mind. So, he didn't notice the man standing at the platform's edge, staring over the ledge as if he wanted to jump. Then, the man came to life. With bloodshot eyes, he spun around. Matthew stumbled. But instead of accosting Matthew, the man approached a light-skinned black girl blocking the law student's path. She started in place as the man said to her, "Trains sure take a long time, don't they?" His lips curled with a coyote's grin.

The girl stepped back a pace. "Yeah... yeah, they do," she stuttered. The man was old enough to be her father.

Matthew didn't want to look the situation head on. He recognized the man. He remembered a story his grandfather had told him about getting his shirt slashed as a young man in New York City simply because he'd interfered in an argument between a man and a woman in the subway. The man had pulled a knife on him. The woman had told the police there was no need for Matthew's grandfather to interfere in their family squabble. So, Matthew righted himself and kept on walking. But out of the corner of his eye, he saw the man proffer a grizzled hand from out his oversized coat sleeve as he said to the girl, "I'm Larry."

* * * *

Matthew would be starting law school in less than a month. He'd just moved to Washington, DC a few weeks earlier. Things felt fresh and invigorating. He'd never lived in a real city before. Moving into the top floor of a converted row house in a neighborhood called Columbia Heights, his roommates had told him to be careful crossing 13th Street at night. One of them had been mugged on the other side of the block. The young man's phone had been taken. Living in the city was awfully different from State College, PA where Matthew had completed undergrad. It was even more different from the York, PA suburb he'd grown up in.

That particular day, a slight breeze swayed the lone tree beyond Matthew's window. From the third floor, it looked a little cooler and maybe even a bit more overcast than DC had been in the previous few weeks, but it still didn't look like rain. So, Matthew gathered up his books for Civil Procedure and Criminal Justice and headed down to the stoop outside to do some reading. He wanted to get a solid jump on his classes. He knew from family, friends, and reputation that soon there would be more work than he could handle, and he wanted to be prepared.

The building's shadow sliced across his stoop. Matthew

positioned himself beneath its shade. Even though it wasn't as sunny as it had been, the day was still bright. Matthew put on his sunglasses. He felt like he cut quite a cool figure out there on his stoop with his books, in his shades with his shirt untucked.

Matthew wouldn't have been able to tell you what specifically he'd been thinking about when the man approached. He hardly noticed him at all strutting down the sidewalk, his chest out, his arms flailing beside him. In jeans and a white tee shirt, with a flannel wrapped around his waist, the black man faded into the city's backdrop, another piece of the urban landscape. He may not have been dressed quite right for the heat, but there was no reason to think he was completely out of place. Not after the things Matthew had already witnessed in his first couple weeks in Washington, DC. However, after mumbling to himself as he walked past Matthew sitting out on his stoop, the man abruptly turned around. He pointed one finger directly at Matthew. "I want to talk to you about racism and gentrification," he said.

As if they'd known one another for years, the man immediately took his place leaning against the handrail leading up the side of Matthew's stoop. Matthew swallowed hard. Not yet used to living in the city, he had no idea how to handle such a sharp statement concerning two things polite company would never discuss. Especially from someone of another race as himself. Matthew answered, "Okay..." But he was taking note of his options for a quick exit if the situation turned violent. There was nowhere he could run to other than back into his building, and that would require getting his key out and having to struggle with the knob on the door. The only real option might be to fight if it came down to it. The black man was smaller than Matthew, who stood a few inches above six feet, which usually gave him the courage to face almost any situation. But the way the man held himself, with his off-center eyes and his narrowed brow as he spoke out the corner of his mouth, gave him the appearance of being quite scrappy. Unlike how he'd always carried himself at college parties, Matthew felt inadequate to the situation. He glanced up and down the street to see if there was a policeman on patrol somewhere who might monitor the situation. There wasn't.

"I grew up in this neighborhood," the man said. "Right around the corner over there is where my mom lived. I went to grade school across the street at that school there. And my aunt, she lived right around the corner, too. My grandma, she came from down the block. And in fact, she used to go to church right here," the man said, pointing at the large, brick building bordering on Matthew's building's property. He'd known it was a church, but it had never really struck him that people might actually attend services there. Even though he'd heard singing coming out of it on the two Sunday mornings he'd lived in the city thus far. It simply didn't seem like the kind of place where you might find spirituality. "This building you're sitting in front of, this used to be the church offices."

Matthew nodded like he already knew that, but in fact, he didn't. "I live here now," he quickly interjected as if that gave him some sort of legitimacy to claim over the stoop.

The black man narrowed his eyes. He cocked his head to the side, but he quickly kept right on talking, "But I haven't been in this place in over 20 years, now. You see, I've been in prison. And things aren't the same here."

At that one word—*prison*—Matthew started in place. His stomach dropped a bit, and he felt a twinge of fear course through his limbs. Images of words he'd heard in gangster movies and rap songs filled his mind, words he'd laughed about with friends in high school and college, words like shank, hooch, broomstick, bitch, and rape. He tried not to look too shocked. He removed his sunglasses for a second and wiped his eyes. He felt a little sick, and he felt like he might cry.

"This used to be a black neighborhood," the man said, and Matthew immediately felt even more uneasy than he had before. "But nowadays, you aren't the only white person living in it. Hell, you aren't even the only white person living on this block. In fact, I bet you aren't even the only white person in that house. You see, I used to *own* this neighborhood. That's why they had to put me away. I was making too much money. So, tell me this… Why is it that the Italians get to have the mafia? And the Jews get to help start Las Vegas? But a black man dealing drugs to his own people, building himself a nest egg for his family has to go to prison for 20 years?"

Even though all his muscles were tense from the man's tone, Matthew shrugged as if this were a perfectly normal conversation to be having at this moment on this sunny Saturday afternoon.

"I'm not proud of what I did to my people, now," the man continued. "But I was an entrepreneur. Just like the people who bulldozed all those blocks down there sometime while I was locked away and put up that Target and all those luxury high rises you and your white friends get to shop at and live in now. I was an entrepreneur."

Finally, Matthew found his voice. "You sure were," he nodded.

The black man looked at him askance. It was like he was reading Matthew's intention from how he held himself on that stoop. Somehow sensing Matthew's sincerity, he went on, "Now, all my people are gone. My mom, my aunt, my grandma, they're all dead. I did 20 years. I got out yesterday. I came home, and I don't have a home to go to anymore. All my people, they're all gone, either dead or moved away. I just came out of prison, and now I'm all alone. You can't take everything away from a man like that. It doesn't matter what I did. That just isn't right."

"I'm really sorry to hear that," Matthew said feeling genuine empathy for the man's situation.

"I didn't ask you to be sorry for me," the man snapped, but at Matthew's blanched expression, he softened his tone for the first time that afternoon, "but thank you for saying so." The black man moved around and sat down at the bottom of the stoop as if he and Matthew were old friends reminiscing about their years together. "They diagnosed me bipolar in prison, you know. They said that's why I did all those crazy things. But I don't know about all that. This was a crazy place back then, and it was a crazy time. I did what I had to do to get mine."

Matthew nodded like he had some sort of idea what the black man was talking about.

"What's your name?" the black man suddenly asked from where he was squinting up at the bottom of Matthew's stoop. He held his hand over his brow to shade his eyes from the sun.

"I'm Matthew," Matthew answered honestly.

"Nice to meet you, Matthew. I'm Larry."

* * * *

It was a few months later, when he was coming home after sharing a couple drinks with some of his new law school colleagues, that Matthew bumped into Larry again. In the distance, he could see a man approach a woman walking past him on the sidewalk. The woman started and paused. She held her hands close to her body before quickly shaking her head and starting off again. The man trundled back dejectedly to stand leaning against a fence, puffing off a cigarette. Matthew saw the thick smoke hanging in the air beneath a streetlight like warm breath on a cool night. Hoping to avoid this apparently homeless man who couldn't be doing anything but spare changing, Matthew crossed the street. When he heard a shout, "Matthew! Matthew, right? It's me, Larry."

Just like the woman who'd been walking a short distance ahead of him, Matthew started in place. Larry bounded across the street after him. "I need help, man," the man said as he slowed to approach Matthew standing slightly buzzed in the fall night.

Matthew didn't extend his hand. Instead, he stiffened in place. He tried to smile. "What's up, Larry?" he asked, hoping he sounded as cool and nonchalant as a man could.

"I need my medication. They're telling me I need to pay fifty bucks for it down at the Dupont pharmacy. I didn't have to do that last time, and I don't have that kind of money. Look at me. I'm out on the streets. I'm hoping to start this job Monday laying concrete, but even then, I won't get paid for another two weeks. Help me out, man. I need my medication tonight. I'll get you back as soon as I get paid. I promise. Word is bond."

Matthew leaned back and rested his hand on the fence behind him. "What's the medication for?" he quite rationally queried as if still discussing the intricacies of case law with his associates back at the bar.

"It's for my bipolar. If I don't get it, I don't know what'll happen to me. I might go off. Who knows. I feel like I'm about to go off right now. I could do something that sends me right back to prison. I don't know."

Once again, it was that single word—*prison*—that Matthew heard loud and clear. Whether he heard that solitary word because of where Larry was afraid he might wind up or what the man might do to get back there, Matthew had no idea. He blinked. He took his hand off the fence behind him, and he stood back up straight. "What do you need from me, then?" he asked soberer even than before.

Larry tensed up. "What do you mean, *what do I need from you*? I'm asking if I can borrow some money." He finished emphatically, "Now, can you help a brother out or not?"

Matthew stood up on his tiptoes. He fished around in his pocket. "I think I might have a five or so in here," he whispered absentmindedly.

"Five dollars? What the fuck am I supposed to do with five dollars?" Larry pleaded. He narrowed his eyes and shook his head.

"Well, how much do you need?" Matthew asked.

"I told you, man. I need fifty dollars."

"Oh, you need the whole amount, then?" Matthew asked as if he hadn't heard the man the first time.

Larry nodded.

"Well, I'm sorry, then. I don't have fifty dollars on me," Matthew said.

"There's an ATM right down the block. You could get that kind of money out of there now, couldn't you?"

Matthew looked around. There wasn't anybody else on the street. He and Larry were all alone. "I'm a student," Matthew told him. "I can't spare that kind of cash."

"Please, man. Like I said, I should be starting work on Monday. I'll get you back. I promise. If you can do it at all, help me out. You're my only hope," Larry pleaded.

Matthew looked around as if there were somebody there to help him make his decision. After nobody responded, he sighed. He asked, "You promise you'll pay me back?"

Larry nodded.

"Because I need that money," Matthew said, trying to judge Larry's sincerity.

"I promise," Larry told him. "I'll keep the first fifty bucks I make right here in my pocket, and I'll come right back here to this street every day where you live. As soon as I see you again, I'll give it all back to you. Every last cent. I promise. I don't want to be beholden to no man."

Matthew shook his head. He really couldn't believe he was about to do this. He was living off loans. He couldn't afford to lose fifty dollars. "All right. Let's go to that ATM," he said. "I'll see what I can do."

* * * *

Larry never did show up to pay Matthew back. By the time Matthew finally saw him again that spring, after a harsh winter, he had completely forgotten about the man and how he owed him money. The lost fifty dollars had never even come up, much less stressed Matthew out. But when he did finally see Larry again, instead of worrying about how the man could have survived that winter—what he must have had to live through: the cold, the snow, the shelters—Matthew simply remembered the money he was owed. But he didn't want to bring that up with the homeless man. Instead, he simply wanted to walk right past him.

Scowling his best urban countenance, Matthew looked straight ahead as he approached where Larry was standing there on the sidewalk in the sun on Matthew's way to the grocery store. Larry's eyes were closed and his face was turned toward the sky. Light bathed his forehead and cheeks. He was wearing dark blue jeans and what looked to be the same flannel he'd had wrapped around his waist the day he and Matthew had met. His lips were moving, but he wasn't speaking to anyone at all. In fact, he didn't seem to be making a solitary sound.

Matthew hoped he could sneak by completely unknown.

But right as he approached, as if sensing Matthew's proximity, Larry's bloodshot eyes opened. He looked straight at Matthew caught completely unaware. Larry smiled with yellowed teeth. It wasn't a friendly smile. It was more like a coyote spotting prey. "I remember you," Larry said.

Matthew nodded. "I remember you, too," he responded nervously, suddenly hoping against hope that maybe Larry had his fifty dollars. "I loaned you that money a few months back," he said. His palms started sweating from the potential confrontation.

Recognition dawned on Larry's face. "That's right. You sure did." His countenance turned more severe. "That's why I want to talk to you right now." He stepped closer to Matthew and grabbed him by his shirt sleeve. "Come here," Larry begged as he pulled Matthew back behind a blue dumpster some construction crew had set up on the edge of the street for the wreckage from the latest building they were demolishing on that block.

The two of them weren't that far off the sidewalk, but they were hidden from the views of most passersby. "I need you to help me, man," Larry said.

As Matthew blinked and braced himself for another financial request, Larry drew a long piece of sharpened metal from out the waistband of his jeans. The knife scintillated in the sunlight. Matthew wanted to cry for help, but all that issued from his throat was a vague squeak. He tried backing away from the grip that had moved from his sleeve to now hold his arm tight, but Larry was a lot stronger even than he looked.

Matthew's stomach plummeted. He didn't have the wherewithal to fight, which was something he'd always imagined himself completely ready to do when confronted by a situation like this. Moreover, he didn't have the wherewithal for flight. All Matthew could do was stand completely still. Holding the blade inches from Matthew's cheek—so the law student had a good look at its edge from the corner of his eye, Larry said, "I need you to throw this thing away for me."

Matthew stuttered, "What?"

"I was just standing there praying when you walked up, man. I was begging the Lord not to make me do what I wanted to do, and then you showed up. And I remembered you. I remembered those times we talked. I remembered how you helped me. And I knew. I need you to throw this thing away for me."

Matthew shook his head. "What's it for?" he asked, not even wanting to know the answer, which on some level he felt like he already knew.

"I don't want to admit to what I was thinking about doing with it," Larry said. "Please, just throw it away for me before somebody gets hurt." He held the knife by the handle and proffered it to Matthew, blade side first.

Matthew didn't know where that knife had been. He didn't know what Larry's plans for it were. His mind was racing. Picturing past and future violence, he thought back to his Evidence class. He said to Larry, "There's a dumpster right there. Why don't you throw it in there right now if you want to get rid of it? I shouldn't touch it."

An almost childlike awe sounded in Larry's voice. "Do you really think I can do that?" he asked. This was hardly the same man Matthew had met over the past summer. He had no idea what had happened to that man in the intervening months.

When Matthew didn't respond, Larry wiped a nonexistent tear from his own eye. As if reading something in Matthew's face that the law student didn't even know he could convey, Larry stared at his terrified countenance. Matthew couldn't meet his gaze. Larry said, "You're right. I should throw it away." He tossed the knife up and into the dumpster.

As the knife landed, falling into the trash with a few slight *pings*, Larry laughed. His sudden gaiety sounded of immediate salvation. He wiped both his hands down his cheeks. "That was a close one," he said, still smiling. "Thank you," he added, and he turned around to walk away as quickly as he'd initially opened his eyes.

That was the last time Matthew had seen Larry before he bumped into him that day on the Metro platform as Matthew was heading home from the law library to pick up some Christmas cards at the Target in his neighborhood for his immediate family. Again, Matthew had never really thought of Larry in the intervening months, of which there had been many, something like eight or nine. He turned as the man said his own name, but he immediately wished he hadn't. He thought Larry might have recognized him from his gaze.

If he did recognize him, though, Larry didn't say anything this time. Matthew wanted to tell the girl Larry had accosted to step away from the man. He was certain he was probably insane, but Matthew was afraid if he did that he might look more like the one who was crazy. People didn't just talk to people on Metro platforms for no reason, and Matthew was no good Samaritan. Plus, the last thing he wanted was any of Larry's attention directed more sharply at him. The man left a pit draining all the feeling from Matthew's stomach. He remembered how physically strong Larry had been and how intense his gaze had always felt. The best way to handle this situation was to keep on walking as if nothing were happening at all.

Do You Even Own Any Red, White, and Blue?

"If I'd known I was supposed to wear red, white, and blue, then I would have." Ralph sighed as if he were observing something as typically depressing as his everyday life. He was wearing a black Pittsburgh Pirates tee shirt, which was a slight nod to his old hometown, an old, black baseball cap and cutoff gray jeans, a regular outfit he'd thought would cut a cool impression with the crowd on this Fourth of July. It would give him the perpetually hip, urban appearance he was looking for to counteract the wrinkles appearing more prominently around his eyes every day.

In a red tank top, blue shorts, and white shoes, Paul, nearly a decade younger than Ralph, bounded along beside him. He responded, "It's no big deal, man. I'm sure other people won't be wearing red, white, and blue either. To get a group of twenty-something DC hipsters all into the same outfit, well, that's like herding cats." Paul was holding his girlfriend, Kim's, hand as they walked.

"I'm not twenty-something," Ralph mumbled.

"Well, you excluded, of course," Paul smiled.

Paul lived in the basement of Ralph's building. Ralph was on the first floor. Smoking cigarettes out on the front stoop, they'd met one another a little over a year ago, when Paul had first moved in. Paul had been single at the time, and even with their age difference, he'd evolved into a good friend. Although, Ralph was in no position to reciprocate. He felt guilty about that. They had a lot in common, including mutual appreciations for music and literature. But more often than not, their friendship revolved around Ralph's complaints concerning this situation or that. He'd been struggling through his thirties (in fact, he'd been struggling for longer than that), and Paul had an understanding beyond his 26 years. It made for good conversations late at night, out on the stoop, smoking cigarettes and drinking beers.

"Who are we meeting up with on the way again?" Ralph asked.

This time, Kim responded, "My friends Julie and Sebastian," she said. "Don't worry. They're fun." For her part, Kim had on a red and white striped dress and blue sneakers.

Ralph was acutely aware of the gray streaks around his temples and his clothing decision from earlier that morning. If they'd still been a block closer to their apartment when he'd first commented on the peculiar patriotism of Paul and Kim's outfits for that day, he would have gone back inside and changed his clothes immediately into something more suitable when they'd told him everybody at the party was supposed to be wearing the American flag's colors in honor of the occasion.

"I wouldn't be so worried if I was wearing red, white, and blue." Ralph sighed yet again as if he actually owned an outfit in those colors. Sure, he had blue jeans and a white tee shirt. But he really didn't own anything in the color red. Maybe, he could have gone out and picked up a bandana or something like that at Target. Money was tight. Ralph had been out of work for over six months already, but he could at least afford to drop a few bucks on something specific to help him fit in somewhere he didn't really know anybody other than Paul. His mom was helping him out with what little she could anyways, which was humiliating to a man of Ralph's age. He hoped nobody asked him how he got by. He needed to make sure he didn't volunteer the information.

"It's really no big deal," Paul laughed.

"Maybe not to you," Ralph mumbled, visibly distressed.

"Really, it's no big deal," Kim said this time. She sounded a little annoyed. "Nobody will care. I promise."

Ralph sighed. Kim's promise didn't mean anything to him. But he tried not to reveal his suspicion. Disregarding her reassurances wouldn't have been the politest way to behave. Besides, he hardly knew her.

Julie and Sebastian were already sitting out on the stoop of Sebastian's building when the existing threesome approached. Sebastian was wearing a red tee shirt, cutoff blue jeans, flip-flops, and a white hat over sunglasses. He took a sip out of a silver flask he pulled from his hip pocket as he stood up. Julie had on a silk-screened American flag tee shirt, which covered all the necessary bases. It didn't matter what else she was wearing. But she also had on red short shorts and ankle-high, black leather boots.

Feeling more out of place than before, Ralph sighed yet again. As if he were a tea kettle getting ready to boil, an almost imperceptible whine escaped his throat. Hoping to catch his attention before that whine spilled into a full-fledged whistle, as if he were a puppy in need of discipline, Kim shot him a quick glance. But Paul seemed oblivious to his older friend's irritation. He introduced his upstairs neighbor to his girlfriend's friends as if nothing suspicious were occurring whatsoever.

Sebastian said Ralph looked familiar. Ralph said he used to work at The Black Cat, a long-time DC club down on 14th Street NW. Maybe Sebastian had seen him there once upon a time. Quickly remembering the potential age gap, however,

Ralph added that was back in the day, though. Nowadays he was a legal assistant. Although, he'd been out of work for a while now. He was revealing too much about himself too quickly. He did that sometimes. He shut up. He tried to still his rushing thoughts and listen. He accepted a proffered sip from out Sebastian's flask.

Sebastian admitted The Black Cat was practically a DC institution. He'd seen lots of shows there in the two years he'd lived in the District, but he also noted they didn't live too far from one another. Maybe, he'd simply seen Ralph walking through the neighborhood before on his way to get coffee or something. Ralph had a particular look, Sebastian admitted. He smiled, which made Ralph even more self-conscious than before. He didn't know what that meant, and he'd thought he looked cool, although fairly nondescript. He didn't smile back. He was thinking how he'd been in the District over 15 years by then, ever since his freshman year at GW, and he remembered how much older he was than Paul, who was older than Kim. Her friends were probably about her age. Ralph didn't volunteer the information that he'd never worked at The Black Cat while Sebastian had lived in the city. He decided he'd better keep his mouth shut. He already wasn't dressed right. The last thing he needed to ruin his holiday was for these kids to realize they were hanging out with an old man.

Ralph looked down. He fidgeted in place. The rest of the necessary introductions and hellos were made. All hands were shaken. Hugs were given, and the group of four plus one continued their stroll down Lamont Street NW from Columbia Heights to Mount Pleasant for the rooftop Fourth of July party they all intended to attend together that afternoon and into the night.

* * * *

They were on the rooftop of a tall apartment complex in Mount Pleasant. From the outside, the building looked like something from the first *Ghostbusters* film. Ralph decided he'd keep that observation to himself, though. The reference might be outdated. It might pin him down to a specific generation, and he didn't want to age himself any more than he had to in the eyes of that rooftop full of twenty-somethings.

A chain link fence penned them in on the roof, kept them away from the building's edge, made it impossible to fall or jump off. Ralph met the host. He worked for Discovery Channel as a video editor for shows Ralph had never heard of since he didn't have cable. He didn't even own a TV. Eventually, the host told Ralph, the fireworks on the National Mall would be visible to them all from up there. When it got dark, they would boom up beside the Washington Monument hazy right now in the heat and distance. But the sun was still out. There was only the loud group of twenty-somethings happily drinking and lounging around on the patio furniture the building provided. And then, there was Ralph.

As expected, he didn't know anybody else at the party. There'd been a time, maybe five years earlier, when showing up at some hipster party in a random DC neighborhood, Ralph might have expected to bump into somebody he'd met elsewhere. But those days were gone. Ralph didn't get out much anymore. He hadn't gotten out much for quite some time. Long hours as a legal assistant had consumed his life for three years, and then, his lack of income—coupled with his worsening depression—had kept him homebound throughout most of that past year. He didn't even want to meet the people Paul was introducing him to. *What are they all going to think about me?* he couldn't help wondering.

He could tell them what his life was like right then—

watching Netflix all day long on the account his mother's money helped him pay for, catching up on all the television he'd missed over the decade and a half he hadn't owned a TV. But he was pretty sure they'd probably all watched *Lost* when it had originally aired, if they were even old enough to do that. His insights from the past few months into programs those kids had grown up with wouldn't carry much social currency in that day's environment. And there was nothing they were saying that Ralph could relate to.

They all had jobs—in government, public relations, and non-profits. They discussed politics with a certainty Ralph couldn't muster. Some of them were musicians or poets, even artists. Whether they made a living at those avocations, Ralph didn't want to ask since his own hobbies currently consisted of smoking too many cigarettes and watching too much pornography. Two things he felt ashamed of as he looked around at the young couples conversing on that rooftop with him. He grabbed one of the beers his host had offered out of the cooler. It was a bottle of Heineken, the only label he'd recognized. He sat down on a stool, alone at a round, chest-high table.

He self-consciously lit a cigarette. The afternoon was bright, and Ralph didn't own any sunglasses. That made him worry about cataracts. His dad had had to have a cataract operation shortly before he'd passed away nearly a decade earlier at only 54 years old. At the thought of his father, Ralph choked up. He thought about putting out his cigarette, but he couldn't. He needed the nicotine too badly. So had his father. That's what had eventually killed him. Ralph took a sip off his beer. He took another drag off his smoke. He tried exhaling in the direction of the fence, but his smoke got caught in the wind. It billowed back over the rest of the party. A young woman wearing the day's requisite colors—a red bathing suit top, blue jean shorts frayed along the bottom, and white sneakers—crinkled up her nose. Ralph was certain it was in disgust at the scent of his tobacco.

From up there, the summer haze hung heavy over DC's rooftops. The distant world shimmered with fluidity. Ralph sat still at that little table, sipping his beer, contemplating the necessity of the fence around the roof's perimeter. Without it, nobody knew the determination somebody like Ralph might make as the day wore on, as he continued drinking in that environment. There was no reason for him to be there, or anywhere, for that matter. He imagined himself falling through the haze, the ground rushing up to meet him, the whooshing world increasing as it came closer and closer to disappearing… Man, that alcohol sure was worming its way into his thoughts. Ralph decided, *I really need to drink more.*

But Ralph wasn't supposed to be drinking at all. According to his doctors, alcohol didn't jibe well with his medications. He'd been diagnosed with depression ten years earlier, right before his father had passed away. But the medications didn't work. In fact, they'd stopped working before Ralph had lost his last job. That might have been part of why they'd let him go in the first place, but Ralph rarely thought about that. Instead, he thought about how he needed a new psychiatrist. He needed a new therapist. He needed somebody to fix him. He'd heard about an organization in the city that helped people with clinical depression reintegrate into society, but Ralph wasn't that bad off. Everybody had down times. There were whole genres of music built around that fact. Ralph had listened to some of them in high school.

"What are you thinking about?" a voice intruded upon Ralph's reverie. One of the twenty-something girls had already slid into place beside him. The girl was wearing sunglasses. She had on the day's requisite colors—a red bathing suit top, blue jean shorts frayed along the bottom, and white sneakers. Ralph frowned.

"Nothing, really," he said. He turned his head self-consciously, and he tried blowing his smoke, once again, away from the girl in the red bathing suit top. But again, the wind caught it and swirled the smoke right back into her face.

"You must have been thinking about something," she said. "You looked super-deep in thought."

"I really wasn't thinking about anything," Ralph lied again.

"Okay," the twenty-something girl said. "If you don't want to let people get to know you, that's your prerogative." She smiled as she spoke, but she didn't leave after she said it. She sat still at Ralph's right, staring at him, sipping her beer with a supercilious lilt to her lips. Then, the edges of her eyes crinkled behind her sunglasses as she said, "Could I at least get a cigarette?"

Ralph hadn't expected that. Fumbling through his pockets, he nearly ripped the top off his cigarette pack as he pulled it from his pocket. He shook a cigarette out for the girl. She took it. "You got a light?" she asked.

Ralph put his lighter up on the table. The girl grabbed it and lit the cigarette herself. She took a drag. She asked, "What's your name?"

"Ralph," Ralph said.

"Hey, Ralph, I'm Laurie." Laurie stuck out her hand. Ralph shook it. As she exhaled again, she asked, "So, Ralph, you want to smoke some pot?"

Ralph's fantasy of climbing the fence and leaping off the roof landed him right back in his chair at that little tabletop. He wasn't supposed to be smoking pot either.

His doctors had told him that, too. Marijuana wasn't such a problem for his medication. According to the doctors, it had stronger effects on his brain's naturally distorted chemicals. But then again, Ralph hadn't expected anyone to take an interest in him at that party, much less someone like Laurie. Out of the corner of his eye, he saw Julie and Sebastian talking to the host. They weren't paying attention. Paul and Kim were nowhere to be seen. Feeling like he was getting ready to partake of a shameful activity, Ralph took another swig off his beer. He nodded, not because he really wanted to, more so because he was lonely and surprised.

"Cool. Let's go downstairs," Laurie said.

* * * *

Ralph was standing atop a boxy structure that stood atop the roof. It housed the stairs from the building leading up to it, but Ralph had already forgotten about that. He'd also forgotten about the chain link fence enclosing the roof proper. The night spread out endlessly in all directions around him. With alcohol and marijuana crossing wires through his mind, Ralph believed he stood free atop the roof alone.

Creating a portrait similar to the artwork for the original *Star Wars* poster, Laurie and some other boy who'd smoked pot with them were reclining against one another at Ralph's feet, sharing a cigarette. In the distance, a burst of red exploded beside the shadow of the Washington Monument. It twinkled out sparks, and a rumbling roar boomed overtop the skyline. Like Rocky at the end of his triumphal climb to the top of the Philadelphia Museum of Art's steps, Ralph thrust his arms up into the heavens as if he were an earthbound Satan trying to punch the angels in their leering faces. He shouted a loud, *Hurrah!* in response to his nation's annual celebration.

He'd gone downstairs with Laurie more so because he

was attracted to her than that he wanted to smoke pot, but he couldn't admit that. It seemed so shallow. Marijuana had never been Ralph's favorite substance. It had an unpredictable effect on him. Sometimes, he enjoyed it. Sometimes, he wound up freaked out in a semi-delusional state, but given his loneliness and Laurie's attractiveness, he decided he couldn't be afraid of the potential consequences. They'd picked up the guy who was sharing a cigarette with Laurie right now on their way down to somebody's apartment. The three of them had wound up in the bedroom there, sitting on a bed taking hits out of a bowl together. The drugs appeared to be just what the doctor ordered, though. Ralph felt better than he had in months. He was thinking maybe he needed to buy a bag of weed for himself. He hadn't done that in years.

To Ralph, it felt as if there were something symbolic about that evening—to be standing high above a rooftop in Washington, DC on the Fourth of July with fireworks exploding all around him. He couldn't put his finger on it, but it meant something. It was like being aboard Francis Scott Key's boat in the middle of Baltimore Harbor so long ago. It was like standing strong through the onslaught of a war, which is exactly what Ralph's life had felt like lately—his own, personal struggle. He remembered the newsreels of Iraq during his nation's "shock and awe" campaign early in the previous decade. He frowned. None of those kids remembered that. They were probably still in middle school then, if that even.

The official celebration was still visible beside the Washington Monument on the National Mall. Families were spread out down there on blankets with coolers beside them that had been drained throughout the day. But fireworks weren't illegal in DC yet. Other neighborhoods were firing off their own in every direction. There went a burst from Petworth. There were some bright lights coming up from Shaw. A red glow exploded in Northeast. The entire roof oohed and aahed. Ralph was certain. This was a symbolic war, and if there was one thing wars brought about, it was change. Ralph smiled. He still couldn't figure out what it all meant, but it felt good nonetheless.

"How you doing?" Laurie shouted up from where she reclined at Ralph's feet.

Ralph nodded. *Fine, fine*, he thought. He squinted through the night. He wanted to figure out where the two couples he'd come there with were. He didn't know if he should still be there if they weren't, and he wanted them to see him. He was having fun. He was fitting in. He wasn't too old. He wasn't too depressed. They never should have judged him. *Did they judge you, or did you judge you?* Ralph caught himself wondering. Then, he forgot. He didn't remember thinking that earlier. But he'd seen it in their eyes, especially Sebastian's. He was certain of it.

From behind them in Columbia Heights, a loud boom ricocheted off the building they were standing on. Ralph jumped in place. The war was coming closer. He caught a glimpse of Paul and Kim at the chain link fence. Paul had one arm draped over Kim's shoulders. She turned and looked up at her boyfriend. As another firework burst above the National Mall, she grew quite beautiful in profile. Paul looked down at her. He was handsome, too. Together, they'd never notice Ralph. They were too enthralled with one another. Ralph looked away.

At that same little, round table Ralph had been sitting at earlier, the same little, round table where he'd met Laurie, Julie and Sebastian were now sitting. They were each in the middle of taking a shot of something. Their arms were bent at the elbows. Their shot glasses were at their lips. The dark liquid looked like whiskey or tequila. As another explosion sprinkled down on Petworth, they set their respective glasses back down on the table. Ralph could tell Julie was smiling. Sebastian leaned back in his chair satisfied. They'd never notice Ralph either. They, too, were too enthralled with one another.

Ralph glanced back down to Laurie sitting at his feet. She was engrossed in a conversation with the guy they'd smoked pot with earlier. They were leaning against one another's shoulders, shouting into one another's ears. Laurie had hardly said anything to Ralph since she'd first invited him downstairs. Ralph didn't know why she'd even done that in the first place. He took his hat off and scratched his head. He put his hat back on and ran his hands down his cheeks. He was alone. In the middle of that party on top of that roof full of twenty-somethings with the entire nation celebrating all around him, Ralph was completely and totally alone.

Loneliness filtered through Ralph's mind. It ran down his spine into his stomach. The pit it left in Ralph's gut sucked his mind deeper into itself. Ralph thought of his father and the pointless cataract operation he'd had a few years before he died. He thought of how long he'd been unemployed already. He thought of the couples he'd come there with and how they'd be going home with one another. He thought of the empty apartment waiting for him alone. Silent as always, he gurgled the black waters of depression. He couldn't escape. He closed his eyes. He walked to the edge. He stepped off. He fell into infinity.

But infinity wasn't very far away. Ralph forgot he was only on top of that boxy structure that stood atop the roof. He hadn't stepped off the roof itself. He forgot there was a fence caging him and the other partygoers in, making it impossible for them to leap. When Ralph landed on the roof ten feet below, he heard a crack. He stumbled. Pain shot through his ankle. He fell to his hands and knees. He rolled onto his back, and he cried out.

Even over the fireworks' booms, the other partygoers on the roof heard Ralph's scream. Most of them didn't know who he was. They'd seen him around. Even though they hadn't met him yet that afternoon. But they saw what he did. Some of them shook their heads and returned to their conversations. Some of them covered their mouths in reflective agony. Others burst out in the kind of laughter human beings can't stifle when somebody else hurts themselves.

Laurie whispered, "Holy shit…" The guy who was sitting with her, shouting into her ear snorted a short laugh. Ralph looked ridiculous rolling around on his back like a beetle who couldn't flip itself over with his face scrunched up like a three-year-old holding back tears. It was his own fault. He never should have walked off that ledge.

Among the couples he had come there with, Julie and Sebastian, still sitting at that table where Ralph had met Laurie, looked at Ralph rolling around on the ground. With fireworks exploding behind them in the distance, they glanced at one another, moved to get out of their seats, smiled at one another and then thought better of it. They were each a little stoned themselves. They'd visited one of the apartments downstairs a few times during the afternoon, too, and they were a little paranoid as a result. The gesture itself appeared sufficient to them. They didn't want to attract too much attention to themselves. Paul, on the other hand, ran over to his friend, while Kim—one hand to her lips—followed at a short distance.

"What the hell were you thinking?" Paul asked Ralph,

who was rolling on the ground, clutching at his ankle. He'd watched his downstairs neighbor walk off that ledge. Ralph had appeared so peaceful, like a monk in meditation before all hell broke loose. It reminded Paul of that video he'd seen in college of the Vietnam War, when that monk had set himself on fire. He'd appeared so full of purpose as he poured the gasoline over himself. Then, as he struck the match, he seemed blissfully unaware of any sense of the suffering either he himself or his viewers must have felt in response to his pain.

Ralph shook his head. "Nothing," he said. But Ralph wasn't that monk. Tears were starting to drip from his scrunched-up eyes.

For a second, as another batch of fireworks sparkled in the darkness over the National Mall, as most of the partygoers forgot about the crazy guy who'd jumped, as they oohed and aahed at the lights in the distance, Paul came to himself somewhat drunk upon that roof. For some strange reason, at that moment, he wasn't sure what was causing Ralph's tears. It might have been the physical pain. It could have been some unseen emotional suffering. Either way, Paul felt Ralph should have been able to remain as stoic as that historic monk.

"I wasn't thinking anything at all," Ralph said.

Isn't It?

They'd only been in the neighborhood since February. It was June. Rob and his wife, Cassie, had moved from Ballston in Arlington, VA to the Anacostia neighborhood of Southeast Washington, DC shortly before their daughter, Eve, had been born that spring. When they realized their lease was coming due only a couple months before Eve herself was due, they realized they could get more space for their money if they bought a home inside the District in Southeast rather than outside the District—but still inside the Beltway—in Northern Virginia. Besides, given the nature of DC traffic, Southeast was even closer to Rob's job in Alexandria, VA than Arlington was. And by Metro, it was a lot closer to Cassie's job on Capitol Hill. It had been a practical decision. With a baby on the way, Rob and Cassie both wanted to cut down on their commutes.

Rob and Cassie didn't know anybody in Anacostia, though. For the first time in either of their lives, they were the only white family on the block. In fact, they felt like the only white family for many blocks. But Southeast was invigorating for Rob. Now that he lived in a predominantly black neighborhood inside the District, he had urban credibility. His colleagues at work gazed at him with wide, respectful eyes. He'd taken a chance moving into Southeast. The quadrant had a reputation. The people who had grown up in the DC area all had their own terrifying high school stories about getting lost in Southeast at one point or another. Rob was a trailblazer. Anacostia was significantly less expensive than either Arlington or Alexandria, and Rob was proud of finding such a great deal inside the District. He'd always wanted to live in the city. Besides, he and Cassie had a backyard, which they hadn't had at their apartment building in Arlington.

Rob could talk with the people at his office about violence in the District and how it affected him directly, which lent a heavy air to his political understanding. He was experiencing things his friends and coworkers weren't. Many of the kids he saw hanging out on the corners were in gangs. He was certain of that. But the neighborhood was changing. The real estate broker had assured Rob and Cassie. They wouldn't be the only white family on the block for long. By the time Eve entered elementary school, the broker told them, the neighborhood—for better or worse—would have an entirely different dynamic.

"Just take a look at Columbia Heights up in Northwest. Or Shaw," the broker said.

Rob and Cassie nodded. They both had known people over the years who had lived in those two neighborhoods. Each neighborhood had come a long way in a short time. Cassie even remembered when she first started at American University in the District back in the mid-2000s, before the Target opened in Columbia Heights, when nobody in their right mind ever went up that far. "Back then, the world stopped at Mount Pleasant," she said to Rob. That had only been a little over a decade earlier. Things changed quickly in Washington, DC. Anacostia would be no exception.

But once Eve was born, the neighborhood couldn't change fast enough for the two new parents. The teenagers on the corners who had made Rob ponder the socio-economic realities of his quadrant now appeared as threatening to him as the neighborhood had sounded to his suburban Michigan mother when he'd first told her he was moving there. He didn't know what those kids did for money, and he didn't know what they might do to him if they knew how much money he and his wife made in a year. Rob and Cassie weren't millionaires, but they made enough that they'd be able to send Eve to private school when the time came.

Then, Rob's car got keyed. He and Cassie didn't have a driveway or garage. They had to park on the street. As far as Rob could tell, none of the other cars on the block had been damaged, and Rob knew it was because he was white. He didn't tell anybody that, but he knew it was the reason. The neighborhood kids didn't like him. They didn't want him there. He'd tried being nice to them when he'd first moved in, but they were so removed. The teenagers glared at him. The younger kids ignored him. Their parents had never introduced themselves to him. It wasn't hospitable. He was surprised they hadn't broken in and stolen his stereo.

That was around the same time the kids started playing in the streets at night. They shouted at one another right outside Rob's bedroom window. School must have let out, and Rob couldn't believe how loud those kids were. He couldn't believe how late their parents let them stay out. They woke Eve up every night, but Rob never said anything to them. He wanted to. They knew he had a baby. He punched his pillow. Cassie asked him to calm down. Rob couldn't believe those kids' parents would let them play so loudly in front of his home when the whole neighborhood knew there was a newborn sleeping in there. If he'd been black, Rob was convinced, the kids and their parents would have respected his family's struggles.

Cassie was still on maternity leave. She had about a month left. Rob was already back at work. He'd only been given 30 days of paternity leave, which everybody assured him wasn't bad. He'd been back at his job since May. The days and nights were taking a toll on him. He was rundown. He was tired. The baby never stopped crying. Even when the neighborhood kids didn't wake her, Eve still ate every couple of hours. Now that he had to be at work at 9:00 each morning, Rob didn't have to get out of bed to feed or change her anymore. Cassie took care of that. But Eve's cries from her bassinet still woke him at least three or four times each night.

Rob would try going back to sleep while Cassie struggled out of bed. She'd never been able to get Eve to latch right. She had to go downstairs and warm up a bottle. Then, she fed and changed the baby before crawling back into bed beside Rob. Startled awake by either his baby, his wife, or the kids in the neighborhood nearly once every hour, it was hard for Rob to get any solid rest. He was starting to worry about his commute. There were bags underneath his eyes. His mind felt heavy. He drank two cups of coffee before leaving the house each morning, but he was still afraid he may not be alert enough to be on a highway like I-295 at that hour. After a full day's work, he was afraid he might fall asleep at the wheel during his drive home. He had no idea what they were going to do once Cassie went back to work, too.

Rob grabbed a beer out of the fridge. He walked back into the living room and settled down on the couch with Cassie to watch some television. She was holding Eve atop the pillow wrapped around her waist. It looked like the baby was breastfeeding, but in reality she was drinking from a bottle Cassie held in her hand. Eve's mouth puckered and sucked. "What do you want to watch?" Rob asked. He was tired, but as long as the baby was awake, so were he and his wife.

There was a Nats game on that night, but Cassie had fallen in love with Bravo's *Housewives* shows since she'd been staying home alone. One of them was on as Rob sat down. He didn't recognize the character onscreen, though. It was a blond woman. He and Cassie had enjoyed watching those shows together sometimes, but that night, Rob wasn't in the mood. Things were hectic at work. He had a lot on his mind. He wanted to watch the game and let himself concentrate on something other than his own life for a little while.

But Cassie had been streaming *Real Housewives* all day long. Things were just starting to get interesting. Two sisters-in-law—Rob could never keep them straight—were angry at one another. It looked like they might even wind up in a physical altercation. Rob scoffed at their bravado, but he didn't have the heart to ask Cassie to change the station. Cassie didn't look at Rob as she said softly, "I'm kind of into this right now."

Cassie's sheepishness annoyed Rob. It always did, but he'd have the whole weekend to empty his mind out. He figured he could spend Friday night at least with his wife doing what she wanted. Besides, the Nats were never going to win the pennant. Rob could check the score on his phone as the evening wore on.

With a smile, Cassie motioned to Rob that Eve was starting to drift off to sleep. Outside, the neighborhood was silent. Rob set his beer down on the coffee table. After only a couple sips, he was already realizing how tired he was, too. The alcohol was coursing through and weighing down his limbs. He whispered, "If you want to put her down, maybe I'll lay down, too."

"I think I'll join you," Cassie said.

Cassie stood up carefully. Rob left his beer where it sat. He might finish it later. Cassie repositioned the baby over her shoulder. Rob clicked off the TV. Cassie placed her hand behind Eve's head so that the baby's neck wouldn't roll, and she carried Eve to their room. The baby had her own room, too, but she didn't sleep in it yet.

Eve didn't always handle the transfer to the bassinet well. More often than not, she woke up screaming. The entire process would have to start all over again. Tonight, though, Rob was tired. The neighborhood, his job, and fatherhood had ground him down. He prayed Eve would stay asleep as Cassie lay her down in the bassinet. Rob loved his daughter already, but fatherhood was more than he'd bargained for.

That night, however, Cassie's bassinet handoff was flawless. Rob undressed as Cassie slid her hands out from underneath the baby. He slipped into a pair of shorts and a tee shirt. Cassie didn't have to get undressed. She'd never stepped out of her pajamas that entire day. The two new parents slipped into bed together without so much as a peep from their newborn daughter. The baby must have been tired. She'd eaten up a storm. Her mouth was still moving in suckling shapes.

Alone beneath the sheets beside his wife, Rob's thoughts turned to sex. He wanted to try and put some moves on his wife, but he didn't know if she'd be in the mood. He didn't want to get rejected that night. They hadn't had sex since Eve had been born. Cassie said she was still too sore. They had to wait a little while longer. Rob believed he was being patient.

The world became fluid and dreamlike when Rob was startled awake by a shout outside. His eyes burst open. He didn't know what had happened. Somebody might have been shot. But laughter followed the noise. Rob realized it was those kids again playing in front of his bedroom window. He closed his eyes tight. Rage boiled in his stomach. All he needed was a bit of sleep. He prayed the baby would stay silent.

Eve awoke with a pitiful yelp. For a moment, Rob thought she might drift back off to sleep. Then, there was another shout outside. Eve let out a blood curdling cry. Somebody might have thought the baby was dying she wailed so loudly. But she was merely waking up. That's how it was every night. Cassie shot out of bed to comfort her baby. Rob bolted upright and jumped to the floor. "That's it. I'm going to go tell those kids what the hell is up," he said. He started walking toward the bedroom door. He didn't even change his clothes.

Cassie's eyes opened wide as she clutched the baby to her breast. "What do you mean?" she asked. But Rob was already out the door and heading downstairs. She didn't know if those kids had guns. She was afraid her husband might get shot. That's why she always begged Rob to stay in bed when he awoke every night enraged at the noises occurring outside their bedroom window. At a slower pace, with the baby in her arms, Cassie took off after her husband.

Rob beat her to the front yard. As Cassie stepped out their door with the baby in her arms, her husband was shouting, "Hey! What the fuck is wrong with you?"

A group of five black kids—three boys and two girls—were looking back at him with blank expressions on their faces. One of the kids was holding a big purple ball like the ones Cassie would have played with in the pool at her grandmother's in California. But there was no pool there. The kids were in middle school, but they looked older to Cassie. Rob was standing a few feet away from them. Trembling from rage, he pointed one finger in their direction, and he said, "You don't like me, huh? You don't like my family? Well, we're not going anywhere. You better get that through your fucking heads. We bought this house.

We live here, and we're not going anywhere!"

Eve started crying again in Cassie's arms. Rob looked back at his wife and baby. He inhaled and puffed himself up even straighter and taller. He towered over the children. "You're probably the ones who keyed my car. Aren't you? It's because I'm white, isn't it?" he said. He shouted at the five middle school kids, "ISN'T IT?"

A light clicked on next door. Somebody stepped out on the porch across the street. Cassie waited for the neighbors to come out and yell at her husband. She was scared one of the kids' older brothers might try to fight him… or worse. But nobody approached their yard. As if the adults, too, were scared of the kids confronting Rob, they merely watched them all—the kids, Cassie, her baby, and her husband. Like her husband, Cassie started trembling, too. But Cassie wasn't trembling from the same rage infecting Rob. She was afraid. She looked back at the teenagers Rob had confronted. She finally noticed the little boy holding the purple ball in his hands was trembling as well. And he was starting to cry.

For It Is in Giving That We Receive

Emily found the Good Samaritan program online. It had been put together by a religious organization, and it had been in effect for over a decade, which made it reputable. Even though she'd been raised Christian, Emily was no longer religious herself. The values, however, remained.

There were only so many charities in the DC area. Emily didn't have many choices. There were two options for adopting a family at Christmas. She could either donate to the family anonymously by dropping off toys for their children at the charity's office. Or she could agree to arrive at the same location at 3:00 pm on December 20th, which was a Saturday, and give her gifts to the children's parents—or parent—in person. Since Emily's own family was a mere afternoon drive from DC, Emily opted for the latter. She had to work until Christmas Eve. So she couldn't head out before then to begin with.

As an attorney in the United States, Emily led a blessed life. Her father was a doctor in Southwest Virginia, which had allowed her to complete her undergraduate education with no loans. She'd graduated from Georgetown Law seven years earlier and had immediately entered her chosen field with a six-figure salary. As an attorney at a large DC firm, she'd worked long hours, but she was now bringing in more than twice what she'd started at with her billing bonuses each year. She'd yet to find luck in love, and she didn't have her own family. But she was only 32 and just starting to get serious with Walt, her newest boyfriend. He'd probably propose sometime in the coming year. For the $1.2 million condo she'd recently purchased in Dupont Circle, she'd received a no-interest loan only available to doctors and attorneys, which was saving her a couple thousand dollars each year.

Emily wanted to give back to her community. It was Christmas after all. Her parents would be proud of her for taking the time and money to give something to the less fortunate. Besides, Emily didn't want to take her lessons from Dickens' Mr. Scrooge. She wanted to show she was grateful for the heights she'd achieved.

At 2:39 pm on December 20th, Emily got into her car with the presents she'd purchased for the family's two children, Miles, a boy, age 6 and Charlotte, a girl, age 4. Since Emily didn't have any children of her own and since neither Miles nor Charlotte requested anything specific, she'd called her brother, Eddie, to find out what she should buy for the kids. The charity's own list of age-appropriate gifts just seemed so boring. They were all either educational or simply bland. A few years older than Emily, Eddie had two kids of his own about the same age as Miles and Charlotte. Of course, for her own niece and nephew, Emily had already gotten more expensive gifts. For the Good Samaritan program, the charity recommended the Samaritans only spend about $25 per child.

For Miles, Eddie recommended Emily get him a particular police dog action figure. His own son liked that one the best. "It comes with a flying net," Eddie said. Emily found the dog on sale online for the right amount. While for Charlotte, Eddie suggested Emily pick up a special kind of doll. His daughter loved hers. It was "The Queen." Charlotte's present cost the same as Miles', and they were both super-cute. All in all, Emily spent about $50, which was precisely what the charity suggested the givers spend. Emily wanted to spend more, though. She wanted the children to be happy. She wanted the children to like their presents.

"But you shouldn't buy them anything extra," Eddie said. "If you get them too much, their parents won't be able to pass the gifts off as their own."

Emily hadn't considered that. She'd never thought Miles and Charlotte's mother would give the gifts as her own, and she felt a pang of regret at the thought of not getting any credit from the children for her selflessness. "But that's the point," Emily reminded herself. "The gift is to give." That platitude satisfied her.

Emily didn't know Northeast DC well, but she didn't have any trouble finding the charity's office. The neighborhood where it was located didn't look too bad, nothing like what Emily feared it might. She'd heard stories about parts of Northeast like Trinidad, but this didn't look like she imagined that would. She wasn't even afraid to get out of her car, which she thought she might be. Even though, as she opened the office's door and double-checked to make sure her car doors were locked, she almost dropped the bag of presents she was carrying. Emily's car beeped, and she felt relieved.

The presents weren't supposed to be wrapped when they were delivered, but since she'd be meeting the mom in person, Emily figured she could simply tell the woman what she got her kids. Emily had spent over an hour the night before wrapping her presents. She wanted them to look cute. She wanted the children's mother to be excited when she first saw them.

Emily had gone down to Georgetown to buy the wrapping paper. That's where she went to buy paper for her own niece and nephew as well. But of course, those presents had been wrapped for weeks. Emily scoured the neighborhood for the right paper—both for Miles and

Charlotte. Miles needed something masculine yet still naive. He was a child after all. Being for a girl, Charlotte's had to be soft and pretty. Eventually, Emily found the perfect designs for each of them.

For Miles, she chose a cream paper covered in pictures of full-grown bears wearing Santa Claus hats. The paper was decorated with a super-cute tagline, which brought a smirk to Emily's lips. For Charlotte, she chose a light pink paper with cherry sprigs decorating it. The red berries with green leaves reminded Emily of poinsettia plants, which seemed appropriate to her for that time of year. At home, Emily already had silky, red ribbons and bows that would go with each paper. Those were left over from the presents she'd already wrapped for her own family.

Making sure not to wrinkle it, Emily carefully creased each piece of paper where she wanted to fold it for the children's presents. She bit her lip as she taped the paper in place with the smallest amounts of tape she could use to make sure the paper was stuck. Then, criss-crossing each one on its bottom side, she wrapped ribbons around the paper and completed each of her projects with a bow. Emily smiled as she admired her wrapping jobs. The presents looked fit for royalty. Even though the children's mother was struggling to get by. She was certain the woman would appreciate Emily's hard work.

Inside the charity's office, Emily introduced herself to the receptionist. She asked where she might find Miss Love, Charlotte and Miles' mother. The lady at the desk said she'd be pleased to lead Emily over to where the woman was waiting. But she also said, as she and Emily headed off, "You know you weren't supposed to wrap the presents..."

Emily nodded, but she explained that she believed the children's mother would be excited once Emily told her what her kids were getting. The receptionist didn't respond.

Miss Love wasn't as young as Emily had expected her to be. She was easily Emily's own age, if not older. Emily found herself wondering what might have happened to the woman to force her into such poverty that she couldn't even afford Christmas presents for her own children. She must have had a job. Nobody could survive in DC without one. And children were expensive. Emily knew that. It was why she worked so hard. She wanted a family of her own someday, preferably with Walt.

Emily smiled. She put out her hand with the bag of presents dangling off her forearm, and she said, "Hi, I'm Emily."

Miss Love shook Emily's hand. "Nice to meet you," she said. She didn't smile back, though. She appeared tired and worn. She didn't seem as interested in Emily as Emily was in her.

"I've got your presents for Charlotte and Miles," Emily said.

As if she'd never heard her own children's names before, Miss Love tilted her head to the side. "Thank you," she said, but she didn't sound like she meant it. Instead of meeting Emily's gaze, Miss Love looked off into space. She sighed before glancing down at the bag in Emily's hand. "They're wrapped?" she asked. She furrowed her brow.

Emily nodded. "Yeah. I figured I'd just…"

"They aren't supposed to be wrapped," Miss Love said. She looked up at Emily. For the first time ever, their gazes met.

Emily flinched. She said, "I know, but I…"

"Let me see them. I need to know what my babies are getting."

Emily handed Miss Love the bag with the two presents she'd so carefully wrapped the night before. She started to say, "I can tell you…"

But with no appreciation for the paper or Emily's wrapping job, Miss Love tore into Charlotte's present first. As she finished pulling the wrapping paper off her daughter's new doll. She turned the box around, held it up, and looked at it.

"You got her a little, white girl to play with?" Miss Love said. "She's going to know that's not from me." She was trembling ever so slightly.

"But..." Emily started to say. Then, she changed her mind. The doll's color had never occurred to her. *Why should it have?* she thought. Turning red, Emily suddenly became acutely aware of her own skin color and Miss Love's skin color as well. Her ears burned. There'd been a black doll, too, she remembered, but Emily had thought "The Queen" was the right one to get. It was the one she would have wanted when she was a little girl, and her own niece already loved it. Besides, why should Emily have assumed Miss Love was black. She couldn't tell that sort of thing from her name or socio-economic status. That would be racist. And what difference did it make if her daughter's doll were white? Emily was pretty sure she'd had black dolls when she was a little girl. And it never would have bothered her. They were one among many of a plethora of races.

Emily remained flummoxed by Miss Love's response. She was trying to come up with something of her own to say when Miss Love pursed her lips and started opening Miles' present as well. As the box was revealed, Emily could see Miss Love's scowl deepen. She finished unwrapping the police dog, and she stared at it with a blank gaze.

"It comes with a flying net," Emily said. Her cheeks were bright scarlet. Sweat was budding on her forehead.

Miss Love didn't respond. She didn't even thank Emily. She looked at Emily like she didn't trust the woman at all, and she stuck both presents back in the bag Emily had given her. Then, she crossed her arms, and she leaned back deeper into her seat. She stared at Emily with an uncomprehending gaze.

After a moment of silence, eventually, Miss Love said, "Neither of those were on the charity's list." She leaned forward and rested her elbows on her knees. She looked like she might cry.

"I figured the list was kind of… restrictive," Emily said. She tried smiling at Miss Love one more time, but the woman still didn't smile back. Emily had already forgiven her for simply tearing into the presents she'd wrapped so carefully, but she was starting to feel a little resentful about Miss Love's lack of appreciation for her dedication and hard work.

Miss Love didn't kowtow to Emily the way Emily would have expected the woman to. In fact, as Emily tried striking up a conversation about the neighborhood where Miss Love lived with her family, the woman grew even more distant than she'd been when Emily had first introduced herself. It was as if she were in a hurry simply to get out of there. It was as if she were somehow offended by Emily's thoughtful gifts. Even though Emily had done the woman and her family a service. Eventually, Emily acquiesced to the desire Miss Love's attitude made so apparent.

When Emily was alone again in her car parked on the street, she wanted to cry. She couldn't believe she'd taken the time to drive all the way into Northeast DC just for that. She couldn't believe she'd taken so much care for everything—the presents, the paper—just for that. She could just as easily have dropped the presents off and never introduced herself to the woman. Then, she never would have known how much Miss Love loathed Emily's gifts.

She'd been so precise about everything. She'd asked her brother for recommendations. If Eddie had been in Miss

Love's predicament—whatever that predicament was—he would have appreciated those kinds of presents for his kids. Emily was certain of that. Miss Love should have been grateful for everything Emily had chosen to do for her family. Without Emily, Miles and Charlotte wouldn't be having a real Christmas at all. Without Emily, there may not have been any presents for Miles and Charlotte to open. Emily was no Scrooge. Miss Love was ungrateful. It was that simple.

The following year, Emily told herself, she wouldn't give gifts to anyone outside her own circle. She shifted her car into drive, and she said as she pulled away from the curb, "So much for trying to be a good Samaritan."

Our Only Hell

Brunch was an impromptu affair when William's mother called again. Just like she had the night before—twice. And just like the night before, William let the call ring through to his voicemail, which he never checked anyway. He needed to remember to give her a call back later. Before he went to work that evening, when he wasn't drinking this mimosa.

At that patio on 11th Street, where Noah and Eileen's presences were simply too enthralling, their laughter too real, their conversation too invigorating, William didn't want to miss a single detail of what was to be said. Besides, right then, Noah was checking his phone to see where they might be able to take a day trip to that afternoon. They'd gotten up relatively early, and Eileen had mentioned wanting to go someplace close enough that William could be back in DC to work by seven that night but far enough away that they could all get a real country drive in for a few hours. It was only one in the afternoon, and she just had to get out of the city for a little while that day. She had a Zipcar account.

She asked William, "Who was that?"

"Oh, just my mom," he said. "I'm sure she'll call back later."

"Yeah, it's probably not that important anyway," she reassured him. "When my mom has something important to tell me, she always texts first just to make sure I pick up my phone."

"Yeah. I figure that too," William said.

"I got it," Noah said. "Let's go to Leesburg. It's only about an hour away. We could totally drive out there, hang out for a bit, and make it back here before William has to work."

"But is there anything to do there?" William wondered.

"I don't know," Noah said. "Probably not, but it's about as far out as we can make it today and still get back in time for you."

"Oh, Leesburg sounds cute," Eileen laughed. "Besides, the purpose of this drive isn't the destination, William, it's the journey. Now, let me make sure I can get us a car…"

Which was no problem, they were on the road within an hour. Pop music bleeped and bleated out the radio, over the wind whipping through William's hair where he sat in the backseat. Eileen was driving. Noah sat shotgun as they cruised down the Dulles Toll Road into Virginia.

All three of them were singing along to the radio's anthem. Perfectly hitting every word in sync with the artist's rhythm, William smiled. It was all so ironic—his friends up front, the picture he must have cut in the back.

The tune ended, and another contemporary classic came on. "Can we switch it up?" William shouted over the wind. "I'm sick of pop music."

But Eileen said, "I love this song." She and Noah went on singing along together.

"You can't be serious," William laughed.

"I am serious," Eileen answered. "This is, like, my all-time favorite song right now." She hardly missed one of the singer's notes.

"But it's total shit," William said.

Smiling, Noah turned around in the front, "Come on, man. Don't take yourself so seriously. It's a good song. You liked the last one. Come on… Sing!"

William smiled at his friend, and he started singing along as well. He knew all the words to that song, too. But his ironic fervor had passed. He craved something that appeared a bit more sincere. Besides, he was no longer certain whether Noah and Eileen viewed the radio through the same prism he did. Even though, he knew the song better than they did.

As they passed the sign marking Leesburg's city limits, William's phone rang again. This time, though, he didn't know the number. It had an 804-area code.

There wasn't much to Leesburg—a couple stop lights, a small commercial district. The three friends were talking about parking and grabbing some ice cream at a corner store they'd passed.

"Jesus Christ, who the hell lives out here?" William asked his friends in the front seat.

Eileen answered, "I don't know. Probably commuters. It's not that far outside DC."

"Yeah, but I mean, what do you *do* out here?" William wondered. "Can you imagine what it's like growing up here? What kind of psychosis do you develop living out in the sticks like this?"

"Oh, come on, William," Noah said, glancing nervously at Eileen. "It's not that bad. Besides, how much different is it from where you grew up in Richmond?" Noah was from Southern California. He'd never been south of Arlington on the East Coast. William's home might as well have been on another planet as far as he was concerned—one that looked exactly like Leesburg.

"Pretty damn different," William told his friend. "Richmond's a real city."

"I never knew you were from Richmond," Eileen said from the driver's seat.

"Yeah, I am," William mumbled.

"I went to college in Richmond. At VCU," Eileen said. "What part of the city did you grow up in?"

"Downtown," William answered.

"Oh," Eileen said. "Like Church Hill? I mean, I know there are other places to live, but..."

"Oh, yeah, sure," William laughed.

"Man, I can't even picture you outside of DC," Noah said.

"I've been here seven years now," William blurted out.

"How'd you wind up here again?" Eileen asked.

"College," William answered. In his pocket, his phone buzzed again.

"Yeah... that sure did you a helluva lot of good," Noah good-naturedly ribbed his friend.

William shrugged. "It's not my fault artists have to wait tables," he said, and he checked the number on his phone.

"*Artists* have to produce something while they wait tables..." Noah whispered to Eileen. She stifled her own laugh.

It was his mom again. *What the hell does she want?* William wondered. He decided he should answer. "Hello?" he said.

But it wasn't his mom even though his phone said it was her home. "Is this Billy?" a woman's voice asked.

William snorted a short laugh at the name he used to be known by. "Yeah, it is. Who's this?"

"Billy, it's your neighbor, Miss Anne. Your momma's been trying to reach you since yesterday. She told me to call you to try telling you to pick up the phone next time she calls. The number will be coming from Richmond. It'll have an 804-area code. Will you answer when she calls? You know she doesn't have a cell phone."

"Sure," William said. Then, he added without thinking, "But why's she calling me from Richmond?"

"There's been an accident," Miss Anne said.

"What? What's happened?" William wondered.

"I'd rather your momma told you," Miss Anne said. "I'm so sorry, Billy. I'm gonna go now. Just pick up the phone when your momma calls."

"Okay," William said, and Miss Anne hung up.

"Who was that?" Eileen wondered.

"My parents' neighbor," William answered. "She says my mom's going to call me. I need to answer the phone. There's been an accident, she says."

Up front, Noah and Eileen looked at each other. "God, I hope everything's okay," Eileen said.

William's phone rang again. It was an 804 number. William answered. "Mom?"

"Billy, why haven't you been answering your phone?"

"I've been busy mom, but I just spoke with Miss Anne. She said something happened. What's going on?" He wanted to ask—*Why are you in Richmond?* But he'd come back to himself in the intervening moments, and he knew he couldn't ask that with Noah and Eileen sitting up front.

"Billy, there's been an accident," his mom said. She sounded distant, somehow cold. "Your daddy's been hurt. Can you come down here today?"

"What? Sure. I can get down there, but where am I going?"

"Richmond," his mom said.

"Richmond?" William wondered. "What are y'all doing in Richmond?" he asked, forgetting himself again, an accent surfacing that neither of his friends in the front seat had ever heard from him.

"He was working up here, Billy. He fell off the roof of the building he was working on yesterday. Your daddy's in real bad shape right now, Billy. He needs to see you. I need you to come down here to Richmond today, to the VCU Medical Center. Will you remember that—the VCU Medical Center? How soon can you be here?"

"I don't know, mom. I'm not in the city right now, and I have to get to the train. That'll probably take me at least an hour, and then, depending on when the train leaves, it'll be at least another two hours from there to Richmond. Then, I'm sure I could take a cab from the train station to where you're at. So, I won't be there until tonight, but—"

"That's okay, Billy. Just get here as soon as you can."

"I will, mom. I promise I will."

"I love you, Billy."

"I love you, too, mom," he said as his mom hung up the phone.

"What was that all about?" Noah asked hesitantly, without turning around, from up front.

"It was my mom," William said. "I need to get to Richmond tonight. My dad's been hurt."

"Oh, God," Eileen said. "It's not bad is it?"

"I don't know," William said. *But if he didn't go home, it must be*, William thought, but he couldn't add that. He swallowed carefully and said, "My mom really wants me to get down there as soon as I can."

"Do you know what happened?" Noah asked.

"He fell off a roof," William said.

"What was he doing on the roof?" Eileen asked.

"He works on roofs sometimes," William answered. "Listen," he added. "I hate to do this to you guys, but I need to get back to DC, like, right now."

"That's no problem," Eileen said. "But," she added, "if your dad's really hurt, and you really need to get to Richmond, it would be a heck of a lot faster if we just took you from here—"

"Yeah, man, I'm cool with that," Noah said.

William looked out the window. "You guys don't have to do that," he said. A redness neither of his friends up front could see slowly colored his cheeks.

"Don't worry. It's really no problem," Eileen said. "I'll just call and extend the car. That's all."

"You don't have to extend the car," William said, rubbing his hands together where they sat in his lap. His palms were starting to sweat. "I can take the train."

"No way," Noah said. "As long as Eileen's cool with it, we're driving you."

"Okay, but I don't know how to get there from here," William said.

"I do," Eileen answered.

"Guess, I better call work, then," William said.

* * * *

Noah and Eileen didn't stay with William in Richmond. Even though they said they were willing to. They both thought their friend might need some support. When they pulled into the loop at the emergency room, however, William thanked his friends, but he insisted they head straight back to DC. He'd take the train back up tomorrow or the next day. From the moment the three of them had pulled off the highway into Richmond proper, William had been saying that exact same thing despite Noah and Eileen's protestations. As they drove away from the hospital with William entering the emergency room's double glass doors alone, they each silently blamed his abnormal behavior on some strange mixture of grief and fear.

Eileen figured she and Noah had driven all the way down there, though. They might as well stop at a little falafel spot she'd discovered during her freshman year at VCU. It would make for a decent outing. Even though it certainly hadn't been on their schedule for the day, but then again, none of what had occurred had been on their schedule. Eileen was from Southwestern Virginia, and that restaurant in Richmond was the first spot she'd ever tasted Middle Eastern food. She thought it might be nice to revisit for old time's sake. Plus, that way she could show Noah a little bit of the city where she'd spent four years of her life.

The two of them had been acquaintances for nearly a year by then, almost as long as Eileen had lived in DC. A friend of hers from college worked at the same restaurant where Noah was a bartender, but they'd just started dating two weeks earlier after a drunken hook up at a random party. The following morning, when Eileen went downstairs to make some coffee in Noah's decrepit row house, was the first time she ever remembered meeting his roommate, William. Although, William insisted they'd met before, but Eileen wasn't sure if William even believed himself when he said that.

The falafel restaurant was a glass structure on a corner. They had to order at a counter in the restaurant's front. Eileen remembered not knowing what *anything* on the menu was and being so confused the first time she'd ever gone there back in college. Sliding into one of its darkened booths in the back, Noah said, "William sure was acting weird, huh?"

Relieved that he had brought it up first rather than her, Eileen answered, her eyes averted as if she didn't want to insult their friend's grief, "I didn't want to say anything, but he sure did."

"I mean, maybe he was just confused because of his dad and all, but it was like as soon as we got off the highway, he had no idea where we were at the whole time."

"I know," Eileen said. With Noah's own questioning, she became more comfortable with the conversation's subject matter. It was as if they were discussing a character on TV rather than a friend of theirs. "It was like he'd never even been in the city before—"

"But he grew up here—"

"I know. Anybody who *grew up* in Richmond should have been able to get us from 95 to the Medical Center. He should've at least known where that's at."

"Maybe he didn't really grow up here," Noah laughed, but he immediately felt guilty for making fun of his friend during his grief.

"Maybe…" Eileen answered, cocking her head to the side.

"I'm just kidding," Noah said. "I know he grew up here. That's what he's always told me, and I've known him for like three years now."

"Of course," Eileen said, but she was starting to wonder. There was something to Noah's theory. She stopped thinking about it. Their falafel sandwiches arrived.

* * * *

In the waiting room, William's mother sat alone in a corner. Even though he certainly didn't want to, not under those circumstances, William still felt an old, familiar disgust well up in his chest when he saw her there staring off into space in her simple shirt and dirty jeans. But there was another emotion tinting his feelings as well. Some sort of grief higher up in his throat. He'd never felt it before. Certainly not in the presence of either of his parents. He walked over to his mother. "Momma," he said.

William's mother's eyes came into focus. She saw her son and stood up to give him a hug. Slowly, William moved to hug her back. "What's happening here?" he asked.

At first, his mother didn't answer. She simply held her

son close. Then, tears burst as she blurted out, "They don't think he's going to make it, Billy."

William refused to understand what he'd just heard. "What's that supposed to mean?" he asked.

"It means the doctors think your daddy's going to die," his mother finished, wiping her nose and eyes.

Then, William refused to believe. The world couldn't change so fast. That morning, everything had been so normal. He whispered, "But that doesn't make any sense." His voice clicked on the last word. His throat was going dry.

William's father was alone in a bright, white room down the hall. Lying rigid in bed, his face and neck were swollen black and blue. The consistent bleating of a heart monitor and the belabored breaths of a breathing machine were the only sounds to be heard. William's father couldn't speak. His eyes couldn't open. William didn't want to think it, but he couldn't help himself. He simply didn't know what he'd come down there for. There was nothing left for him to do other than silently say goodbye forever to that man who could no longer even hear him. William was trying not to, but he was crying. His father didn't know he was there.

Back in the waiting room, William asked his mother, "How'd it happen?" He was wringing his hands together in his lap. His hidden accent was getting thicker with each word spoken. Noah and Eileen would hardly have even recognized the sound of his voice anymore.

His mother said, "Your daddy's been coming up here for work a lot lately. There's not much construction going on back home right now, but here in Richmond... He's been spending the night during the weeks and coming home on weekends. He's been working on this hotel over on what they call Main Street. I don't know quite what happened to cause it, but yesterday afternoon, he slipped off one of the rafters real high up. I guess he couldn't catch himself. He fell a few stories. They say he probably knocked his head on one of the beams coming down. When he landed, he wasn't moving. He wasn't talking. They got him in an ambulance and took him straight here. The foreman called me. I came up early this morning. I didn't even know it was as serious as it is. I tried calling you, but you weren't answering. Why didn't you answer, Billy?"

"I was busy," William mumbled.

"What were you so busy doing, you couldn't even answer your own family? It's what I always tell you. You've got to answer us in case something happens."

William shook his head. "I was busy," he mumbled again. He saw himself the night before after he finished his shift, sitting at the corner of a darkened bar, trying to talk up the girls who'd gotten there before him and were already well on their way to having too much to drink. He shook his head to clear the vision.

"You're always too busy," William's mother sighed in exasperation.

William's father was taken off the breathing machine that night. Too much damage had been done in the fall. He was broken all over. It certainly wasn't something William wanted to think in the moment, but he would have said that about his father even while the man was still alive. He was a broken-down model, an outdated prototype of a human being. At a mere 47 years old, William's father was already something that had no place in the world, which is why William so rarely visited, why he never told anybody where he was actually from. The mustiness of his family's home might be palpable. If he wore it on his sleeve, others could sniff it out, and William would be in danger of them noticing him as obsolete as well.

The morning after his father died, William and his mother left Richmond. The long drive south was peppered blue and green, but William didn't see any of it even though he stared out the window the whole way down. He hadn't slept much the night before. They'd stayed in the waiting room, not wanting to shell out money for a hotel. There was a lot to be done now that his dad was gone. William didn't want to admit it, but his life was going to change. He couldn't keep waiting tables in DC and working on his "art." His mother needed help. She hadn't worked full time in years. Below a tinge of sadness, rage about the uncontrollable silently boiled. William needed to open his kettle-like throat to let off some steam, but he had nothing worthwhile to say. They drove in silence.

When they finally made it back to William's childhood home, he couldn't believe he was standing on the threshold of that dead world once again. The stoic trees were tired and old. Every time he left, he swore he would never return. Every time he returned, he swore it was for the last time. Entering what was now his mother's home alone, he recognized the foreign scents that had come to represent his parents' lonely lives. Noah and Eileen might have found the smell inviting, but William would never know. The earthen spice curdled in his stomach.

William and his mother were speaking only in terse comments. Their statements conveyed information alone, no feelings. They were too emotionally distant from one another in their physical proximity to embrace the moment's power, leaving them internally numb, sensitive only to the world outside as evidenced by William's mother's muttering of the single word, "Damn," upon her brushing up against the wall on her way to the kitchen to boil some water. Without another word, William went straight to his childhood bedroom.

His bedroom door creaked upon its hinges. It hadn't been opened in long enough that his father had stopped bothering to spray it with WD-40. William twitched at the thought. He inhaled the must that had collected across his debris over the years that room had been left vacant.

The untouched world appeared a time warp. A stuffed toy lion from his early childhood stared at William from out the corner. It was dirty and worn, and it hadn't been there when William had last opened the door. How long ago had that been? He couldn't recall the lion's name. Even though it was on the tip of his tongue. A couple old toys fought a battle across his dresser. William had no recollection of ever having set that up. He had no recollection of the last time he'd even seen those toys from his childhood. His mother must have placed all that there sometime to selfishly remind herself of William's youth, or maybe William's father had done it. William inhaled heavily. The door had been closed for a long time.

There, on the corner of his dresser. He'd forgotten all about it. He certainly hadn't expected to see it when he'd opened the door. He vaguely recalled when his father had given it to him as a gift when he'd graduated from college. It was a black timber wolf William's father had carved himself from a single piece of wood when he'd been 22—the same age William had been when he'd finally received the gift. Only, William's father had started carving that wolf while he'd waited in a hospital for his son to be born. The wolf was snarling. Its coat bristled with power. William had never even brought the wolf back up to DC with him. Its ancient artistry meaningless, William had lost the wolf as soon as he saw it. Somebody must have found it, though, and left it right there for him in his old bedroom. As William made his way over to the tightly fitted sheets he'd dreamt between throughout his childhood, he picked that wolf up off the corner of his dresser.

William lay down on top of the tucked-in covers of his old bed. He remembered the heavy sensation of the comforter beneath him overtop his spindly 10-year-old legs. Those covers had been waiting a long time for a child to crawl between them again, but that day still wasn't the day. As if he wanted to force the reality of its presence back into his heart, William held the figure of the wolf tight against his chest. He rolled over onto his side as he'd done on many a childhood summer day. Somehow, he'd forgotten all about the heart his middle school self had carved into his bedroom wall. Inside the heart, the words "*I love Summer*" were still written in black magic marker. Nobody had ever erased them. Nobody had ever painted over them. William could barely remember what any of it meant.

Embracing the Devil at the Heart of This World

"So tomorrow night, then?" Jodi said through her phone from the other side of the city. The trace of her accent, a subtle remnant from nearly 15 years earlier, was slightly evident. That meant she was already getting a little nervous.

"I'll be there," Charlie responded while staring out the wide window of his fourth story apartment onto the street scene below. The commuters coming from the Metro had thinned out, and the city appeared populated by its native inhabitants.

"Okay… And you're sure you don't want to get together tonight, then?"

Something twittered inside of him, but still, he said, "No. Not tonight…" As he imagined Jodi's body lithely wrapping around his own in the way that, in his experience, only she could do… "I've got work to do, and besides we'll probably spend the whole weekend together anyway." He smiled with the corner of his mouth as he said it, though she couldn't see it, though he found himself suddenly quite seductive.

Which Jodi appeared to have sensed all the way across town as she answered, "Well, just remember, lover boy, tomorrow night you meet my parents. You have to be on your best behavior around them. No offense, but they're not exactly thrilled I'm dating a white guy. But my little sister… you don't need to be on good behavior around her. She's such a little brat, you'll love her. I wish she could come out with us after, but you know… *c'est la vie*. You're not nervous, are you?"

"Not at all. I'm actually looking forward to it," he responded, which he was, in a sense. Although, he wasn't looking forward to driving all the way out to Virginia to do it, but that was their agreement, and he and Jodi were definitely at a point where this was appropriate. Even though he couldn't believe it had all happened so fast.

"All right, then... I'll see you tomorrow," she said.

"Yep. See you tomorrow," he responded.

"I love you."

"Love you, too."

"Good night."

"Night..." And Jodi was off the phone. Charlie had work to do, and he wasn't quite sure why that whole conversation couldn't have taken place over text. There was a grant proposal due tomorrow morning, to be submitted to USAID by the end of the day, and although his research was already done, Charlie had to write it still. It was 7:30 in the evening, and he hadn't even eaten dinner yet. So, Charlie turned on his laptop, ordered some food online, pulled up his notes, and sat down to write.

A little over two hours and a single cup of coffee later, to his surprise, Charlie was pretty much done. The proposal hadn't taken nearly as long as he'd thought it would. He wanted to believe he was getting better at his job, but the truth probably lay in the caffeine, which was also the reason Charlie was pacing circles around his apartment, walking from his kitchen up to the large walled window and staring out at the pedestrians strolling down 14th Street. He should have told Jodi he'd stop by later.

He could have called her then, but he didn't feel like it. Like he'd told her, he knew they would spend the whole weekend together, and that night, Charlie was really enjoying his time to himself. His mind was crisp, and his thoughts were flowing freely. As if he were on the cusp of some great insight, the whole sensation reminded him of his undergraduate years. He decided it might be a nice night to take a walk.

Outside, the air was just starting to get warm and moist, a precursor to the types of evenings Charlie had first spent in DC nearly a year ago before he and Jodi had even met. Not quite sure where specifically he was going, he decided to head down 14th Street in the direction of the National Mall. Although, that would certainly be too far to walk, Charlie pretended to himself that's where he was heading.

When he got to U Street, however, his intention changed. The stylishly dressed, carousing crowds appeared to be enjoying themselves freely arm-in-arm stumbling against one another. Charlie wanted to be a part of all that. He veered left off 14th and entered among the wayward wanderers exploring that night.

He ducked in and out between the black, white, Hispanic, Asian, and interracial couples and friends exploring the intricacies of their city's life. Not quite sure where he was going, Charlie kept his eyes glued and his ears tuned to the darkened bars he strolled past, wondering if maybe he should duck into one and grab a drink to celebrate his early finishing of that work proposal. He felt like a champion of some sort, and he knew that something as simple as a single drink could keep that feeling coursing through his limbs throughout the entire night. Yes, he wanted a drink to cap off his walk. Just one and he would go home—an early night, back to bed and work the next morning. He certainly didn't want to be tired or hungover when meeting Jodi's family the following evening.

It was the music that attracted Charlie's attention—the

heavy techno thump with its high, electronic squeal punctuating the bass. A single heavyset bouncer stood beside the empty ropes and open doorway leading down to the darkness. Charlie had no intention of entering a club of any sort that evening—just one drink and he was going home—but when he stopped and cocked his head to listen, the bouncer instantly told him, "Free before midnight."

"Really?" Charlie asked, certain there must be a catch.

"Yeah, man, go on in." The bouncer nodded to the steps Charlie could then see descending to the pumping music's source. And since it was free, Charlie figured it was as good a place as any to grab the drink he really was starting to look forward to that evening.

* * * *

In the darkness, amid the flashing lights, the bar wasn't very crowded yet. It was probably for the best. Charlie knew he had to get home early, and the sparsely spaced patrons standing and sitting around proved to him already he wasn't dressed quite right for the occasion. A club hadn't been on his schedule. Maybe, he should have switched out of the khaki pants and button-down shirt he'd worn to the office that day. Maybe, he shouldn't have come in at all. Regardless, he was there. He sauntered up to the bar and ordered a beer.

Dancing had never been Charlie's thing, and electronic music was definitely something he didn't really have much experience with. When he did go out, the bars and dancehalls he tended to frequent were littered with pop hits. Charlie leaned against the wall beside the DJ booth and gazed through the darkness at the few dancers making their way onto the floor. One couple was already nuzzled together, probably on their second or third stop of the evening, which must have started right after work. But what really attracted Charlie's attention was a group of four girls in the corner across from him. Already dancing in a tight circle, they looked a little too young to be there, or maybe, at 27, Charlie had finally grown old.

One of the girls, in a pair of tight jeans and a shimmering backless blouse, broke away from her group. She turned and started walking toward the bar, straight in Charlie's direction. Slender and brown, wearing a stud through one nostril, she was probably from the same region of the world as Jodi. An exoticism that had always attracted Charlie—but that he could never mention to Jodi even if he himself were actually aware of it—fluttered in his chest. Warmth oozed through his guts. As the girl made brief eye contact with him, he thought he discerned a slight smile lifting her lips. Feeling both her youth and his girlfriend made his ogling inappropriate, Charlie came back to himself. He took a sip from his beer and glanced into the flickering darkness, but he basked in the girl's fresh scent as she brushed past close enough even for him to feel the wind off her shoulders.

That was when Charlie decided he needed to get a second beer… even though he wasn't done with his first one yet. There was no reason for him to go home quite so early. He'd had a busy week, and he didn't want to walk off the beginnings of his comfortable buzz simply to be kept awake at home by the lingering effects of his earlier caffeine consumption.

By the time that second beer was done, though, Charlie figured he should grab another one. Then, he decided to cap off his night with a whiskey and soda. He rarely went out drinking by himself, and the club was really starting to fill up. It would be a shame to leave right as people were beginning to finally pack the place, and Charlie hadn't even started dancing yet. By the time he got his second whiskey, the electronic rhythms were starting to filter through his body, spurting out his stuttering legs through footfalls gyrating across the barroom floor. With each sip off his stiff drink, Charlie moved one step closer to the dance floor and one step closer to that group of four girls still grooving together in the corner.

Flapping his arms in time to the beat, Charlie was on the dance floor before he knew quite what was happening. His drink splashed over his fingertips. He licked them. The flashing lights were brighter out there, and he felt more a part of the evening's frivolity. Casting lighted reflections that felt like his own mind, a disco ball spun above his head. Crowding around his jerky momentum, more individuals and couples packed themselves onto the floor. Charlie wasn't as self-conscious about his outfit as he'd been earlier. Even though he didn't mean to, he kept one eye trained on that younger girl with her friends in the corner.

She had a field of gravity about her, and Charlie felt himself magnetically drawn toward her presence. An oblivious air wafted from her vicinity. Two unknown guys, provocatively twisting their hips with shirts unbuttoned down their chests, saddled up beside the girls to be ignored. A pang of jealousy Charlie knew he had no right to split his guts. His drink wandered through his mind and watered his synapses. He licked his lips. The world spun in time to the lights and music. Before he knew it, Charlie was thrusting his awkward way into the girl's proximity.

With every twist of her neck, Charlie thrilled at the scent from the young girl's hair, a glimpse of her profile. He wanted her to, but he didn't want her to, notice him. Then, she spun around and faced him. Charlie hadn't even realized how close he'd been dancing to her. Her wide eyes lit at his proximity. Knowing he didn't mean to but hoping to maintain her attention, Charlie tried moving his hips in time to hers. She smiled, and he was certain it was at him and not his awkwardness. He smiled back.

Setting his empty glass beside them on a table at the dance floor's edge, Charlie leaned forward and against any sober judgment, shouted over the electronic din, "Can I buy you a drink?"

She shook her head, pointed to the black X marking her hand, and without missing a beat said, "Not old enough…"

When she threw one arm loosely over his neck and took another step in his direction, Charlie realized he'd stopped dancing. He had to recover his beat or leave. Such a subtle provocateur, the whiskey wormed its way through his thoughts. He put his left hand on the young girl's hip, drew her body closer to his, and tried once again to mimic her tight rhythm.

She didn't move away from his grasp. Unlike Charlie, she didn't seem to think there was anything wrong with them dancing together. Charlie took this as a good sign. Without meaning to, he tightened his grip about her waist.

The two of them ground closer and closer together. Charlie felt their breathing more and more in sync. His brain floated lightly submerged in whiskey. Then, he didn't know where it came from. Like the American Revolution, he had no idea who started it. At that exact moment, he had her cheeks cupped tight within his palms, and he was forcing his tongue between her lips.

"*Come home with me*," he found himself whispering as she retreated from his grasp, one of the other girls clutching at her arm, pulling her away from him. Her wide eyes staring…

Charlie became aware of himself standing still on the dance floor. The crowd surged all around him. The girl spun away to be sealed against his embrace by a backward wall of her three gyrating friends. Charlie blinked. He shook his head and scrunched up his eyebrows. The liquor dissipated with the same force as its initial onslaught. Charlie didn't wait. He quickly sidestepped his way off the dance floor. He ran up the steps leading down into the darkness, and he ducked back out into the warm night.

* * * *

"It's nice to meet you, Mr. and Mrs. Gupta," Charlie said as he sat down for dinner at that Italian restaurant with Jodi the following night.

"It's nice to finally meet you, too," Mr. Gupta said as he took the seat directly across from Charlie at their circular table. Jodi was on Charlie's left. Mrs. Gupta was on his right. The seat between Jodi and her father was left vacant for Ari, Jodi's younger sister who was still on her way.

"Jodi has told us so much about you," Mrs. Gupta added once she was seated.

"Ari should be here any minute," Mr. Gupta said, checking his watch. "She's coming from Maryland. We can order dinner then."

As they awaited Ari's arrival, the conversation got off to a slow start. Jodi was talking across Charlie to her mother about some familial matter involving aunts and cousins. Mr. Gupta was staring at his menu, which was actually for the best. Even though he hadn't meant to, Charlie had definitely overdone it the night before—a handful of drinks in only a few hours, not in bed until after one, awake at seven, a full day of work, and then, there was that young girl twisting behind Charlie's closed eyelids every time he blinked…

"Ah… there she is," Mr. Gupta said, closing his menu and standing up again. The whole table rose along with him.

When Charlie turned around, it was obvious Ari recognized him as well, and Charlie wondered if the rest of the table could tell. Ari paused mid-step. Charlie shifted uncomfortably. The vision haunting him all day had appeared there in the flesh. With a quick flick of her neck, Ari regained her composure. While Charlie wanted to run from the situation but couldn't.

Jodi stepped forward and hugged her little sister. "Charlie, this is Ari," she said with excitement. And as Ari extended her shaky hand toward his, while staring at her wide eyes and the stud through one of her nostrils, Charlie became certain she was the same young girl from that club the night before.

"You look so different in person," Ari told him once their palms touched.

"Yeah, so do you," Charlie mumbled.

"Where have you two been checking each other out?" Jodi laughed. Neither of them responded, not even a grin. The party seated themselves at the table once more.

Mr. Gupta ordered a bottle of wine for the table without consulting with anybody else about what they would like to drink. "But you can't have any, young lady," he told Ari, which Charlie had already assumed would be the case. Jodi's little sister was barely 18 years old—seven years younger than Jodi herself. What in God's name had she been doing in that club last night? Charlie had a blurry memory of her showing him the black X on her hand. It wasn't that he was getting old. She really was young. Charlie swallowed slowly and tried settling into his chair, which was impossible given the present situation.

As the waiter poured the bottle out into four glasses for the drinkers, Mrs. Gupta noticed, "You are being awfully quiet tonight, Ari. Is everything okay?"

"Oh yeah," Ari said distractedly, "I've just been studying. I've got a lot on my mind right now."

"I figured you were tired from being out at the clubs all week," Jodi joked. "I mean, you'll be back at Mom and Dad's for the summer soon. I'm sure you don't want to miss out on any prime dancing time while you're still in the dorms."

Mr. Gupta glanced sternly in Ari's direction. "I don't go out to clubs," Ari told her father, but Charlie was certain she glanced at him as she spoke.

"I was just kidding, dad," Jodi said. "We all know Ari just wants to sit on campus and study. She never goes down to U Street… ever."

"What is U Street?" Mrs. Gupta asked.

Charlie winced. So did Ari, but nobody else seemed to notice. "Nothing, mom," Ari said.

"Oh, it's this block of clubs in DC. Not too far from where Charlie lives. I'm sure Ari doesn't know anything about it." Ari shot a quick glance across the table at Charlie, which easily could have been misinterpreted. But Jodi was simply trying to pull her boyfriend into the conversation. He'd been awfully quiet so far that night. "If Ari wasn't studying all the time, she'd probably be checking it out though," Jodi added.

"But you can't do anything there," Mr. Gupta said. "You're not old enough."

"Of course I'm not old enough, Dad," Ari said. "That's why I don't go there."

"I was just kidding anyway," Jodi smiled. She squeezed Charlie's hand, but he didn't respond.

There was some discussion about what everybody was ordering, which Charlie participated in politely. Once everybody's mind was made up and the order was taken by their waiter, Jodi said, "If you'll excuse me, I have to use the restroom." She set her napkin to the side and stood up.

With hardly a pause between them, Ari stood up as well. "Me too," she said, and she followed her sister to the hostess stand where, presumably, they asked where the bathroom was.

Charlie followed their simultaneous departures with his gaze.

With the two girls gone, Mrs. Gupta asked him, "So, tell us again what you do, Charlie."

Trying to find some words, Charlie stumbled over his thoughts for a minute. Eventually, he said, "I work for a non-profit that specializes in South Asian issues." But that wasn't at all what was on his mind at the moment.

"What sort of issues in particular?" Mr. Gupta wondered. "There are a lot of issues in that part of the world," he knowingly laughed. So did Mrs. Gupta.

"Um…" Charlie really wanted to excuse himself. He wanted to get out of that restaurant and go home before the two sisters came back. But he was in Virginia, and Jodi had driven them there. There was no way back to DC without her. *I could call a cab*, Charlie thought, but by the time a cab got there, Jodi would have already returned from her conversation with Ari. Somehow, Charlie managed to tell Mr. and Mrs. Gupta, "Currently, we work primarily on issues of domestic and sexual violence."

"Very important issues," Mr. Gupta said.

But Charlie was having a hard time tracking their current conversation. Instead, he was picturing the exchange the two sisters were probably having right then over the wash basin in the women's restroom…

So, um, I've met Charlie before, Ari says.

Oh yeah, where? Jodi asks…

"And where did you go to school?" Mrs. Gupta was

asking him.

"Excuse me?" Charlie said.

"Where did you go to school?" Mr. Gupta picked up for his wife.

"I did my graduate work at Tufts," Charlie responded.

"In Boston," Mr. Gupta said, "excellent school."

"It's in Medford, actually," Charlie absent-mindedly corrected Mr. Gupta.

"Oh. I always thought it was in Boston," Mr. Gupta said.

"Close enough," Charlie responded.

"And how long have you been in DC?" Mrs. Gupta asked.

"Almost a year," Charlie said.

When Jodi and Ari came back, without a word, they quietly slid back into their places at the table, which went silent upon their return. "Well, don't stop talking on my account," Jodi said.

Charlie glanced from his girlfriend to her little sister and back again. At his second look, Ari subtly shook her head, *No*. But Charlie didn't know what that meant. When dinner was served and nothing had been said about his and Ari's interaction the night before, Charlie still wasn't sure what that meant. When their plates were cleared, the dessert menu brought out, and still nothing had been said, Charlie didn't know what any of that meant. And as they sipped their cappuccinos while discussing Charlie's upbringing in suburban Chicago, he still didn't know what anything meant.

It wasn't until his drive home with Jodi that night that the world finally began making sense again. Albeit, in a whole new way.

"So I think that went pretty well," Jodi said.

"Yeah?" Charlie asked.

"Yeah, I can't believe how talkative my parents were with you. They've never liked me dating white guys… But maybe they're finally starting to realize we aren't in Delhi anymore. It only took 15 years…"

"What did you and Ari talk about when you went to the bathroom?"

"Oh, nothing. She told me not to tell my parents about U Street anymore. Apparently, she was there last night."

"Oh," Charlie said. "What was she doing there?"

"Probably just dancing—"

"Did she say anything else about it?" Charlie wondered.

"No," Jodi said. "Just that she went out to some club there and doesn't want Dad to know about it. She's afraid they won't let her live in the dorms anymore if they find out what she does with her free time."

"That's all?"

"Yeah. That's all. Why?"

"I don't know. She didn't say anything about me?"

"Yeah, she did," Jodi said. Charlie swallowed slowly. This was the moment he'd been waiting for. "She said you seem really nice, which I'm sure everybody thought since you were so quiet. Were you really that nervous, or are you just tired? I mean, how late were you working last night? You've been really subdued all evening."

"Hm? Yeah, I guess I'm just tired. Maybe I was a little nervous, too. I worked pretty late last night," Charlie said. And as he finally settled deeper into the passenger seat of Jodi's car, he found a new sensation arising within him, a sensation that felt like it must have been latent in him all his life but that he'd never allowed himself to indulge in before. It wasn't relief. It wasn't security. It wasn't accomplishment. And it wasn't pride. Somehow, it felt like some strange admixture of all those things. He didn't have a name for the sensation, but he embraced it, nonetheless. It felt powerful. He knew he wanted to feel it again, and he knew he could. He simply had to figure out how to make that happen.

And I Will Make You Fishers of Spare Change

"*Please, help me. A dollar... A quarter... A dime...* Anything..." Beneath the afternoon sun, the kid didn't seem to know what he really needed. He simply knew he needed help. He was hounding the commuters up and down 14th Street. Most of them didn't pay him a moment's notice. They kept their faces straight as they click-clacked away from him. His fingernails were long. His skin was ashy. His hair—unkempt. His shoes were falling apart. Neither his shirt nor his pants fit quite right. A dirty sweatshirt was tied around his waist, and he kept scratching a spot he couldn't quite reach on his back. There was desperation in his eyes.

The kid was a relic, a ghost, a remnant from another era most of that day's commuters didn't know about. Even the kid himself, at 22 years old, had only heard stories about those days, before there were restaurants and boutiques dotting that block, when his uncle got shot in the neck at 14th and V—the same corner the homeless kid was hounding passersby at right then, right in front of a new restaurant that had popped up a month or two before. His uncle didn't die from that wound, though. He was still alive, fresh from 15 years in prison, clean and sober in Alcoholics Anonymous and living in a shelter in Southeast DC. The kid, however, was neither clean, sober, nor living in a shelter. It hadn't come to that for him yet. His uncle had tried talking to him some, but the kid wouldn't listen. He had his own ideas.

Despite what his mother had told him, the kid believed there was another way. He hadn't formulated that idea very succinctly yet. He never formulated anything very succinctly, but on some level, he believed he could get by and still do what he wanted to do. He could sleep in alleyways and scrounge up enough change to eat and not go to prison or get beaten to death on the streets. Those were his ideas.

But right then, his ideas were making him desperate. Maybe, he wouldn't get beaten to death, but he very well may starve on that same block that was lined with restaurants to eat at. All you needed was money the kid didn't have. So, unlike most of the commuters assumed, he wasn't begging for change for drugs or alcohol. He needed to eat. He'd been so sick for so long, he hadn't even considered food since he didn't know when. Now, his stomach was so empty it felt like his body might rip in half. His legs might crumble away from his torso as a gust of wind split his intestines in two.

There was a 7-11 up the block on the next corner. That's where the kid wanted to go. He only needed a couple bucks to get a hot dog from there, just a dollar more to get two. And it was rush hour. The sidewalks were more filled with people than they'd been since that morning, but nobody was willing to stop and help the kid out. So, he kept running alongside the commuters, begging, "Help me, please. A dollar... A quarter... A dime... Anything..." That's when, from across the street, Dave noticed the kid's lack of success.

Dave was on his way home from work. He'd just stopped for a moment to light a cigarette. As he dropped his spent match onto the sidewalk, he noticed the kid across the street, and he developed a theory. Dave worked in PR. He wrote email campaigns for a firm on

K Street, asking people to give their money to this or that cause or candidate. He convinced people of what they thought might be true, and he capitalized on their convictions. As he took his first drag off the cigarette he'd just lit, he smiled a bit at a thought that popped into his head. Then, he walked across the street to strike up a conversation with the kid.

The kid didn't see Dave coming. Searching up and down the block for a potential mark, he was licking his lips, biting his nails, rubbing his stomach, paying attention only to himself. Too obsessed with the food he needed, he couldn't see the opportunity approaching. People's views grow myopic when they're in pain. They turn inward and focus on survival. The world beyond themselves exists only to serve them in ways they're afraid it may not. It wasn't until Dave, casually smoking his cigarette, had almost run straight into him that the kid finally whirled on the man. With wild eyes, he begged, "Please, help me. A dollar… A quarter… A dime… Anything…"

"I can spare a cigarette…" Dave said.

The kid nodded.

"… And some advice," Dave added as he pulled a cigarette out of his pack and handed it to the kid. The kid cocked his head to the side. He looked askance at Dave as he stuck the smoke between his lips. Dave pulled out a match and lit the cigarette for him. The kid took a drag. With the nicotine in his system, he calmed down a bit. He exhaled. The hunger didn't disappear, but being acknowledged by another made his situation feel more manageable. He took another drag.

Dave said, "Look, I make a living writing letters asking people to give me their money, which, it seems to me, is pretty much the same thing you're doing out here. Now, I'm good at my job. I make a handful of people a lot of money.

So, I thought maybe I could give you some pointers on how you might be able to make more money for yourself with this whole thing you're doing right now."

The kid glanced sidelong at Dave. He wasn't in the mood for a lecture. He needed food, not advice. He'd already left school a few years back. He needed a helping hand, not some guy's perspective. He definitely wasn't interested in anything Dave might think about the world. The guy even admitted he had a job. The kid looked away, but he kept hanging around because he still hoped there might be some money at the end of everything.

Dave said, "So, what's your name?"

"Michael," the kid mumbled.

"No kidding," Dave said. "That's my name." Michael looked back at Dave. His eyes opened a little wider. He stepped closer to Dave, but Dave laughed. "Not really," he said. "My name's Dave, but I got your attention, huh? For that one second, you related to me. And that's all you have—one second to get somebody on the hook. But that's also all it takes—one second to get somebody hooked. You see what I mean? I know what I'm talking about. I could really help you."

Dave's metaphor resonated with Michael. He felt like he'd played that game before. Only he'd always been on the receiving end of the line. Like a fish who'd fallen for the worm one too many times, he rubbed his tongue along the inside of his mouth as if he could physically feel the scars from all those intellectual and spiritual hooks. He focused more closely on the cigarette he was smoking, and he opened his mind a little to what Dave had to say.

"Listen, I see you running up and down this street, chasing people back and forth, begging them to help you, and you're not getting anything. Am I right?"

Michael nodded.

"That's why I'm here to teach you how to fish. You see, you gotta dangle a line for these people. But first, you gotta figure out who's hungry. Nobody wants to eat if they aren't hungry. I'm sure you know that. Take a look at them all walking up and down the street."

Michael looked. He wasn't sure what Dave was talking about, but he sure was hungry. Everybody appeared the same —white or black, in suits or casual outfits—none of them seemed interested in Michael's disheveled appearance. None of them cared about anything related to him. Some of them made eye contact with Dave, but they avoided Michael's line of sight as if his vision carried a contagious disease, as if they might wind up in his same predicament if they acknowledged his existence.

Dave continued, "They're just trying to get home. They don't want to help somebody who looks like you get whatever you're trying to get. So, don't go chasing everybody. Wait until somebody notices you. Then, dangle your hook. Getting somebody to give you their money is like Judo, man, not Karate. You want to use their own weight against them to help them fall in the direction they're already leaning. Make them feel special about being the person you're talking to. Tell them, 'You look like somebody who might be willing to help.' That gives them a purpose. Everybody wants a purpose.

"Then, if they look a little more closely at you right when you say that, ask them if they can spare one second to help the homeless. It will really only take a second, you'll tell them. Now, you've given them—not only a purpose—but a cause they can believe in—homelessness. Think about it. These people live in DC, man. They don't want to help an individual. They want to help a cause. 'Think locally, act globally,' if you remember the old saying, that is…

"Now, if they stop and are still willing to listen to you, you tell them specifically what you need. Not 'a dollar, a quarter, a dime, anything...' You tell them you need three dollars and 17 cents to get somewhere specific. Tell them you're trying to raise money to get back home to Baltimore to see your daughter, but you're three dollars and 17 cents short. The oddity of that specific number makes it sound more realistic.

"No, you tell them, you don't need Metro fare. You're willing to walk to Union Station. That'll make them think you're willing to put your part into the transaction. You just need the MARC train fare. You're sure if you can just get that specific amount from them, you'll be able get home. Most of the people will still say no. They might give you a few quarters or dimes, but you'll be surprised by how much some of the ones who say yes might actually be willing to part with. I'll bet you get eighty percent of your profits from only about twenty percent of the people you talk to.

"When they start reaching into their wallets, then, you tell them you used your last bit of money to get here to DC to find out about a job, maybe as a janitor. But your buddy lied to you. The man wasn't hiring. You've been stuck here sleeping on the streets for over a week now, and you're just trying to get home to Baltimore to be with your daughter again. She's staying at her grandmother's, and their phone was turned off since you're out of work.

"See what I'm doing here? I'm still giving these people something they can believe in. They're not helping you. They're helping the janitor they feel guilty about having overlooked in high school. They're helping themselves by helping build the world they want to believe in. Do you follow me?"

Again, Michael nodded.

"All right, then. That's all the change you'll get from me today, man. Go fish."

Dave walked away without giving Michael a single cent, but he believed he'd helped him.

As if he'd been in a trance, Michael shook his head. He watched Dave disappear around the corner up the block down Florida Avenue. His stomach grumbled once more. He touched his hands to his abdomen. He was hungry, and he didn't know if the man's plan would work. But it couldn't treat him any worse than the rest of that day already had. Trying to ignore the mind-numbing pain in his belly, Michael licked his lips and stood up straighter. Narrowing his eyes, he gazed intently at the passersby, looking for a potential mark, a commuter who showed a modicum of interest in his situation. They all averted their eyes.

Then, one woman in the midst of the crowd made eye contact with him. She didn't stare. She didn't look for long at all. She merely glanced in his direction, but Michael pounced. He tried remembering Dave's first lesson. He blurted out, "Could you help save the homeless?"

The woman didn't stop walking. She didn't say anything in return. But she did turn her head a little bit more, and she did gaze at Michael again for a little while longer as if she were finally bearing witness to some vague apparition manifesting before her.

That was the most attention Michael had received all day. His pulse started racing. He tried remembering what Dave had taught him. His words tumbled out overtop one another as if they were competing for air. He said, "I'm just trying to get home to Baltimore. I'm stuck down here, you see. And my daughter, well, she's back in Baltimore, and she's sick. I've been stuck here for a week. That's why I look like this. I don't have any money for the train fare back home. I've been sleeping on the streets. I came down here to see a man about a job, as a janitor. I only need three dollars…"

Before Michael finished speaking, though, the woman had already opened her purse. Michael was in awe, he stopped talking. The woman reached into her purse, and she pulled out a dollar, a whole dollar. When she handed that dollar to Michael, he felt dumbstruck. He tried to thank her, but even though his lips were moving, his throat wouldn't produce a sound. But it didn't matter. As soon as the woman handed him that dollar, she started walking away again without even looking back at him. She obviously wasn't thinking about what she'd done. She didn't seem to care about what she'd done. She'd merely acted, and now it was over. It had happened as if she were a robot whose string had been pulled.

For a second, Michael smiled. Then, he shoved that dollar deep down into his pocket, and he kept his eyes glued on the passersby, waiting for the next person who might notice him, however subtly that might be. He was hungry. But after Dave's lesson, he was already halfway to a hot dog in no time flat. His stomach growled at the thought. He'd already spent half the day on that corner, and he hadn't collected so much as a nickel before. Dave had been right. He needed to pay attention to the commuters. Things were serious. He didn't want to miss an opportunity.

After a number of people walked by him and after another handful of people still ignored him when he spoke to them, Michael's next prospect gave him a five-dollar bill. A freaking five-dollar bill. Now, that was crazy. Michael walked up the block immediately to that 7-11. He ordered two hot dogs. He put relish, ketchup and mustard on each of them. He didn't get the 40 oz.

he was already salivating over. He wanted to save the money he had left over to see how much he could actually pull together. He didn't want to, but he was afraid he might head over to a trap house that he knew about up in Petworth. And he knew, if he did that, he'd need as much money as he could get. He licked his lips. If he could pull enough money together, he might just do it. There was nobody telling him he couldn't. That money was his to do with as he pleased. Most of the people walking past him on the street had no idea they could score so close to where they lived or worked. They had no idea there were junkies nodding off so close to them. A mere 15 dollars would get Michael a bag that could take him away from this place for a good little while.

He was so broke. He spent more time sick than he did high. After the last time he'd finished detoxing on the streets, he swore he'd never go back. It had been horrible, shaking and sweating and vomiting for the last two days in an alleyway beside a dumpster in Shaw. The stench was overwhelming. Its memory still turned Michael's stomach. He was only going to drink alcohol going forward. But with the angle he'd learned from Dave, he was considering scoring a bag once more. He was willing to take a chance on having to detox on the streets once more, and besides, Michael told himself, nobody cared anyway.

Michael kept up with the same line Dave had sold him on. He made some more money as evening wore on, and he kept right at it as nightfall approached and the same commuters started heading back out to the bars. Before he knew it, as the stars shone bright above Washington, DC, he had another ten bucks nestled safely in his pocket. He felt good, better than he'd felt in weeks. He picked up a half-smoked cigarette butt from across the street where he'd originally started, and he made his way up 14th Street through Columbia Heights and into Petworth.

Before he knew it, he was knocking on the door of a yellow house he'd been to more times than once. The guy who opened the door didn't have his gun visible, but the look in his eyes made you believe he could probably reach it pretty quickly. With a nod to the doorman, Michael stepped inside. It was obvious they knew one another.

No, he hadn't robbed somebody, Michael laughed along with the guy who held out the little brown baggy to him in the palm of his hand. But it was true. He hadn't had 15 dollars to score with in a long time. He'd been splitting bags and rigs with other addicts after they'd pooled a day's or a week's money together for as long as he could remember. They were usually sick and shaking, sweating and trying to count out how much they each had between themselves. The same guy who was selling Michael that bag today would usually shake his head as they tried bargaining with him for more than the amount they had dictated they should get. Michael probably already had HIV, but he didn't like thinking about that. Tonight, though, the whole bag was his. Tonight, the whole bag was going into his arm alone.

He left with a warning from the doorman about how far away he needed to go before he shot up, what would happen to him if he didn't heed the man's advice. Michael decided to be patient. He didn't feel very sick anymore. With the bag and the rig in his pocket, he walked all the way down to Malcolm X Park. It was a pleasant night, and the park's natural scenery was enticing. Michael stopped at a liquor store on the way and grabbed a lighter and a bottle of Mad Dog 20/20 with the few bucks he had left. Since it was already dark, he settled into an alcove beside the steps below the Joan of Arc statue. Nobody would see him down there. He could fix himself up with impunity.

Without taking it out of its paper bag, Michael took a few swigs off the bottle of Mad Dog. The sweet flavor scorched his throat. He set the open container down beside himself in the corner. He made sure it was easy enough to reach if he needed it, and he cooked the entire bag up in its cap, licking his lips the whole time. He never did take another sip off that bottle.

The next morning, as the sun shone through the trees, two little boys out on a walk with their mother cried when they found Michael dead with the open bottle undrunk in a brown paper bag beside him and the needle still sticking out of his arm.

Johnny and Bruce Were Friends

Johnny and Bruce had been good friends in middle school, but they'd lost touch over the years. Back then, they'd attended the same school, and they were both metalheads, which was a middle ground between their two cultures. The music brought them together. Being from different neighborhoods in a county just south of Richmond, in high school they attended different schools. By the time they graduated, they'd lost touch and taken their one-time commonalities in different directions. Johnny had turned into a punk while Bruce had further embraced his blue-collar roots. Johnny was on his way to college, and Bruce was starting a career driving trucks. Nearly two decades later, Facebook brought them back together.

Facebook had brought a number of people back into Johnny's life. He didn't think much of it. As an adult, he'd gone from Richmond to New York, all the way out to Los Angeles and back to the East Coast for law school in Washington, DC. Other than traveling the country's highways as a truck driver, which allowed him to see a great deal of his native land, the only move Bruce had ever made was one county farther away from the city of Richmond itself than where he and Johnny had grown up. While Johnny had grown increasingly urban over the years, Bruce had settled into a rural life Johnny knew nothing about. Having already retired from the road, Bruce owned a truck repair shop. He was married with a young daughter and a grown stepson. Johnny lived in DC with his current girlfriend, Annabella, who was of mixed race and a decade younger than him. She was closer to Bruce's stepson's age than either Johnny's or Bruce's. Johnny was in his final year of law school at American University when Donald Trump was elected president.

Two days after the election, Johnny got a message from Bruce. The message read—*Hey man, it's been a long time for sure, but there's some things I need to talk to you about. Do you have any time for that? Thanks, Bruce.*

Johnny wasn't thrilled with the idea of talking to Bruce right then. His old friend had posted support for a trucker's strike against Obama during the 44th president's administration. Johnny never understood what the protest was supposed to be about. It was shortly after the Occupy movement had shut down in Manhattan. Everybody was organizing a grassroots protest about something. The goal had been to shut down traffic on DC's beltway by driving semi-trucks shoulder to shoulder. Apparently, that would usher in a general strike throughout America. Nothing came of it.

Johnny messaged his old friend back with one word—*Sure*. He knew Bruce must have seen his posts over the years voicing support for socialized healthcare and other liberal causes. The two old friends decided they'd catch up by phone that Saturday. They exchanged phone numbers. It would be the first time they'd spoken in 25 years.

At their basement apartment in Petworth, as he was getting ready to head down to Malcolm X Park to make the phone call, Johnny told Annabella, "Yeah, I don't know what this conversation is going to be about or how it's going to go. Back in middle school, Bruce wore a jean jacket with a Confederate flag sewn onto the back. I didn't think anything of it at the time. It was pretty normal for the culture I was surrounded by, but by the time I finished my freshman year of high school, I never would have had a friend sporting that kind of symbol."

Annabella nodded. It always made Johnny nervous to discuss what he was like in middle school with her. He could tell she was already upset.

For some reason, though, in defense of his old friend, Johnny said, "Of course, though, back then, along with inverted crosses and upside-down pentagrams, I also used to draw swastikas on all my school book covers. So, I guess I shouldn't take anything Bruce did in those days too seriously either. I'm sure he's changed over the years just like I have. But in middle school, I was only trying to be as offensive as I could be. Bruce was expressing his own beliefs. I don't have any idea what he might want to talk about today."

Annabella said, "Well, either way, it isn't a conversation I'd want to have right now."

Annabella hadn't been in a good mood since she woke up to the election results that Wednesday. She'd spent the first two days crying about Trump's win and the day and a half since enraged at everyone and everything. She'd been betrayed by her country, she'd told Johnny. She hadn't believed the United States was still so backward, but she should have known better, she later admitted. As a light-skinned black woman, she'd often been mistaken for white, which meant she'd heard many things white people would say that were never meant for a person of color's ears.

Johnny walked down to Malcolm X Park for his conversation with Bruce. He'd have more privacy in public than anywhere in the one-bedroom place he shared with Annabella. As soon as he set foot in the park's verdant space, he pulled his phone out of his pocket, took a deep breath, looked back at Bruce's number from the message, and dialed it.

The other line rang only once before a voice Johnny recognized from his distant past answered, "Hello?"

"Bruce?"

"Johnny," Bruce said, and Johnny could hear a smile creep into his old middle school friend's voice.

"Yeah, man. How are you doing?"

"Oh, I'm all right," Bruce said. "It's been a long time, huh?"

"Yeah," Johnny said. "Something like twenty-five years."

"Wow, man. That's crazy."

There was a pause during which Johnny pictured Bruce looking off into the trees probably in the distance. Maybe there was a shed out there, too. Johnny had little more than a vague idea about how Bruce might be living. He asked, "So, what's up, man. Why'd you need to talk to me?"

There was another pause on the other end of the line. Then, Bruce said quickly as if he expected Johnny to shut him down any second, "I want to start a nonprofit, man, and I thought you might know something about that. What with you living up in DC these days and everything…"

Bruce stopped talking. Johnny stood still for a second. His mouth opened, but he didn't respond. That wasn't something he'd expected Bruce to say to him. He'd been ready to defend his beliefs against his old, conservative friend, but he wasn't prepared to give him any advice.

When Johnny didn't respond, Bruce said, "I am right, right? You do live in Washington, DC, don't you?"

Johnny stared at the Washington Monument rising through the gray sky in the distance. He said, "Yeah, I live in DC. But, I mean, what kind of nonprofit are you thinking about starting?" He imagined Bruce wanting to form some sort of conservative PAC. He had no desire to help his old friend with that.

"I want to start a nonprofit to bring this country back together. I thought maybe you could help me do that."

Bruce's response took Johnny by surprise again. "I'm not sure if I understand," he said.

"Look," Bruce said, "I know you and I don't see eye to eye on much politically these days. I've seen your posts over the years, but I think if we just talk to one another like we're doing now, we might find we still have more in common than we have differences. Does that sound right to you?"

Johnny nodded even though Bruce couldn't see. Then, he said, "Maybe."

"See," Bruce went on. As he spoke, Johnny could tell his old friend had thought about this a lot over the past week, ever since the election, ever since he'd first reached out to Johnny. Bruce said, "I've never been much on politics myself. Sure, I have my opinions and beliefs like we all have, but then, with this election..." he paused, not so much for effect, but rather out of necessity. He had to gather his thoughts.

"I have a friend," Bruce finally continued, "or rather, I had a friend, I guess. She's a lesbian. I've never cared one way or another how she chooses to live her life. But the day after the election, after Trump won, she unfriended me. She didn't even ask what I really thought about anything. She simply said she couldn't be friends with somebody like me anymore. Just because of who she believes I voted for. That really hurt my feelings."

"Yeah," Johnny said. He looked down at the sidewalk upon which he walked. He didn't agree with how Bruce had phrased that one sentence—*how she* chooses *to live her life.* "I'm not surprised, though," he said. He didn't add how many people he'd thought about unfriending after the election—members of his family, his own parents.

Bruce continued as if Johnny hadn't said anything. He was so focused on getting his thoughts out into the open and into his old friend's mind. He said, "So, what I want to do is start a non-profit that brings people like you and me together to talk about things, people with really different political views from one another. I was thinking we could meet once a month. You choose people you know with your beliefs, and I choose people I know with my beliefs. That way we can all see what we have in common rather than simply reading all over the internet how different we all are. Maybe, these kind of meetings could pop in other cities if they go well for us here. What do you think?"

"Sounds interesting," Johnny said. He was thinking.

Bruce continued, "It's the sound bites we get that tear us apart. I really believe if my lesbian friend had just talked to me, she'd have seen where we see eye to eye instead of only how different a vote for Trump and a vote for Hillary are. That makes sense, right? I mean, we're all still Americans, aren't we?"

When Bruce finished his plea, Johnny didn't say anything at first. He exhaled deeply. He was standing at the top of the park beside the statue of Joan of Arc. It was a monument from the women of France to the women of America. The figure rose above the concrete. Astride her horse, she stared at the heavens. She held her sword aloft. It forced Johnny to realize something he hadn't wanted to admit to himself yet. He said, "I don't know, man. I don't know if it's that simple."

"What do you mean?" Bruce asked.

Given the version of Johnny Bruce had known in middle school, Johnny was hesitant to have this conversation with his old friend. He was embarrassed by how far he'd gone as a youth in his attempts to offend people. Sometime in seventh grade, he'd come up with the theory that everything which was bad had to be good and everything which was good had to be bad. It made for some twisted reasoning that wasn't in line with Johnny's core values. Back then, he'd expressed ideas about race and gender that still turned his stomach. He hung his head. He said, "I don't think it's that simple, man."

"Why would you say that?" Bruce asked.

Johnny exhaled heavily. Even though he'd turned his own middle school beliefs around, he didn't believe everybody could do that. Annabella often complimented him on how willing he was to learn from other people. *Not everybody's like that*, she reminded him. Johnny said, "Because these divides are deep, man. I don't know if you understand how offensive Trump's rhetoric has been to large portions of this country. It's not just that people don't agree with his positions. They feel like he's threatening their right to be…"

"But I felt that way under Obama. I got over it. Just because your guy loses the election doesn't mean you need to hate everyone who voted for him."

"This isn't just a question of losing an election. People are genuinely scared about what all this means for their existence."

"Can't you see, though, Obama didn't do my people any favors either. I own a truck repair shop, you know, and the price of diesel is so high right now my customers are thinking they might have to get off the road. That's their living, man."

"I'm sorry to hear that, but Democrats don't control the price of gas."

"They tax it, though, don't they?"

Johnny didn't know what to say to that. He was afraid his next words might come from a place of his own privilege.

He exhaled and gathered his thoughts. He said, "Gasoline taxes are a good thing, though. I mean, I don't know anybody who drives the highways for a living. So, I'm not seeing the immediate effects, but higher diesel costs encourage people to consume less petroleum, which is good for both the environment and international politics. The environment needs fewer fossil fuels burned so our children have a world to live in—"

"That's up for debate," Bruce said. Johnny had heard that same argument from more conservative members of his family. He chose to ignore Bruce's comment.

"And the international balance of power is heavily weighted in the direction of petroleum-rich countries, which aren't known for their stellar human rights records. I mean it's mind-boggling how the United States can support a regime like Saudi Arabia's—"

"Now, that's something we can agree on," Bruce laughed.

"But it's because of oil. Not to mention, the amount of wars this country has been involved in over the past decade as a result of our addiction to gasoline. What do you think Iraq and Afghanistan were invaded over? It certainly wasn't 9/11. I mean, Afghanistan, maybe, but Iraq, come on, man... I think it might even be a good thing if we could convert every engine on the roads to something more sustainable like biodiesel or electricity or something like that."

"But my clients can't afford 'something like that.' And tell me, who's going to fix those new engines for them? Everything is computerized nowadays. So, it damn sure won't be me. I'm no computer programmer."

"I'm sorry to hear that, but the world's always changing. We all need to adapt to compete."

"And to make matters worse, even with my job right now, my stepson already can't afford health insurance. And that means—under Obamacare—he has to pay a penalty now, too. We're drowning in bills over here, and my son requires medications we simply can't afford. I respect what Obama was trying to do for this country with the Affordable Care Act, but it's just not working."

Again, Johnny didn't know what to say. He wasn't in the same position as Bruce. He didn't have a grown stepson, and he didn't have to pay out of pocket for health insurance anymore. His was provided by his school. But he did remember the current incarnation of the Affordable Care Act wasn't what Obama had originally intended. He said, "If I remember correctly, it was House Republicans who watered down that bill."

"But it was Obama's idea. He owns it. They only did what they had to do to implement it. Look, I'm all about trying to help people out, but I've got to worry about me and mine first, and we're barely keeping our heads above water."

"Insurance wasn't affordable before Obamacare, though, either. I went without through most of my twenties because of that. Luckily, I never got sick. It would have broken me and my family. The Affordable Care Act isn't perfect, but it's a helluva lot better than anything we've had before, in my opinion."

"And in my opinion, it's more of the same," Bruce added. "You can only push people so far before they get afraid they might break."

At Bruce's words, something snapped inside Johnny's head. He realized what had been at the edge of his thoughts ever since their conversation had started. He said, "But there are already people in this country who aren't afraid they might break, they're broken. You want to talk about taking care of you and yours, there are whole areas of major

American cities that don't have access to grocery stores—"

"I didn't know that."

"Yeah, they're called food deserts. And rents are so expensive in some of these places—my girlfriend and I pay over $2,000 a month in rent for a one-bedroom, basement apartment in a not-so-great neighborhood—"

"Jesus—"

"That the people who grew up here can't even afford to live near their families anymore. They can't afford to live near the public transit they need to get to work. And forget about buying a place. There are neighborhoods in this city where the homes already sell for almost a million dollars. And that's not because those places are great. It's because the developers can get that kind of money from somebody who works in PR down on K Street rather than at the Walmart on Georgia Ave. It's gentrification, man. The properties in somewhat desirable, traditional minority areas are bought up by wealthy developers and rented out for more than they're worth to white suburbanites like me. Because we're dumb enough to pay these kinds of rents since we want to live in a city so badly just to fulfill our adolescent fantasies. And DC isn't even the most expensive city in this country. Not to mention the overbearing police presence making sure *I'm* safe while profiling my neighbors of color who grew up there—"

"I never heard about all that."

"Yeah, well, on some level, that's what the struggles in Ferguson and Baltimore were about, and that's hard living, man. Electing a billionaire real estate baron who's known for screwing over minority tenants is definitely not the answer to those problems.

"And don't even get me started on what Trump's

rhetoric throughout this past election means for people who aren't white. My aunt always says the man can't be racist simply because he's a New York businessman. He needs to be accepting of others to make the deals he makes to survive, but I tell her she needs to spend more time in New York City. Minority business owners aren't the majority there, and you definitely don't need to respect someone you're planning on screwing over.

"My girlfriend—who's mixed race, by the way, which means she's black—has spent this entire past week terrified about what all this means for her and her family. She's wondering if she's even still safe in her own country. And until she starts feeling like maybe people don't want to hurt her simply because of the color they've decided her skin is, no, I don't think there's common ground for a conversation between the two poles of America."

Now, it was Bruce's turn to be silent. Johnny stood still in the middle of Malcolm X Park, wondering if anybody was staring at him and thinking about the conversation they'd overheard him having. He was breathing heavily as if he'd been exerting himself.

Bruce sighed, "That makes me sad, man," he said. "I really want to believe there's something we can do to bring this country back together again."

Beneath the city's gray sky, Johnny frowned. Rising higher than any of the many buildings in DC's skyline, the Washington Monument still towered in the distance. Today, that ancient phallic symbol resembled a man in a pointed hood. Johnny wished he could share Bruce's desired optimism. His old friend had grown into an even better man than he'd ever imagined he could be. Johnny wanted that thought to bring him hope, but instead, he said, "I don't think we can."

We're Really Going to Do Some Damage Now

*K*yle *didn't know what to expect at the meeting.* The PR firm he worked for, Greenlight Media, had been bought out by Adolfson, a much larger firm, nearly a year earlier. Adolfson didn't make any changes to Greenlight at first. In fact, the first time Adolfson's officers came to give a presentation, they said they wanted Greenlight to keep running along as it had been. They'd strutted around Greenlight's conference room and repeated the mantra of "business as usual." In their straight-backed chairs, Greenlight's employees clapped. They were relieved.

When Kyle had first joined Greenlight nearly three years earlier, the firm had been a successful PR agency for over 25 years. Never one of the largest players in the space, Greenlight still had a long pedigree and a once distinguished list of clients. Kyle was excited to go to work for them. There was no reason—Adolfson said—to make rash changes simply because the firm had fallen on hard times and ownership had changed. Kyle's manager was thrilled at the announcement. Back at his desk, he said to Kyle, "We're really going to do some damage now." Then, he went back to shuffling his papers.

That introduction had been held nearly a year earlier, though. Greenlight had yet to see its fortunes turn around. Adolfson had already paid off Greenlight's existing debts, which had kept the company tied tight for years. Kyle had always been told not to take any risks. In meetings, he'd brought up ideas, but they always got shot down. Creditors were watching their every move, he was told. There wasn't any space to make a mistake. Greenlight couldn't get approval on financial investments, and it was hard to grow their business with no outside investments.

The company's backend systems were all outdated. They had great employees, Greenlight's officers and managers always said, but their technology was shit. They needed some breathing room to really grow the business. Adolfson had updated their backend systems. They'd floated them a $1,000,000 loan for further investment in the business. Greenlight had breathing room, and the firm still hadn't managed to grow their roster of clients or their bottom line. When Kyle sat at his computer, looking over the numbers from his latest campaigns, he knew Adolfson couldn't be happy with them.

Those thoughts ran through Kyle's mind as he took the Metro from where he lived outside the beltway in Springfield, VA to Adolfson's DC office. They made him nervous. Kyle didn't take the Metro often. Greenlight's office was in Old Town Alexandria. Usually, Kyle drove to work. But that day was different. Kyle straightened up in his seat as he stared out the Metro car's windows at Northern Virginia sliding past before the train ducked into the tunnel after National Airport and barreled on toward Crystal City and the Pentagon. Luckily, Kyle didn't have to make any transfers from the end of the Blue Line at Franconia-Springfield—the closest Metro station to his own home—to the heart of downtown DC where Adolfson was located in a massive office building at Farragut West. He stared out the window as the electronic music streaming through his phone disappeared. There wasn't any cell service in the tunnels beneath the city. With a frown, Kyle pulled his earbuds out of his ears and kept thinking about what might occur at the meeting he'd been invited to attend.

The meeting was a monthly meeting held by Adolfson's copywriting staff. Since Kyle was one of four in-house writers at Greenfield, the new parent company had invited him to attend as well. Presumably, someday he'd be attending that meeting regularly. He was one of Greenlight's few copywriters, and although Adolfson said they intended to keep Greenlight's operations separate, Kyle hoped he'd have the structure and support of the parent company behind him. Greenlight's struggling writing team could certainly use it.

The three other writers from Greenlight—Katharine, Todd, and Jay—were meeting Kyle at Adolfson's office. Each of them was coming in separately. None of them lived in DC proper. Still in their mid-twenties, Katharine and Todd were both junior writers. Jay was older, however. Nearly 40, he was even older than Kyle, and he was more experienced. He'd worked at some big agencies before settling down at Greenlight a number of years before Kyle had arrived. Greenlight was Kyle's first agency, he'd worked as an in-house copywriter for a printing company before switching to Greenlight. It had been his dream to work in an agency setting. And even though he'd originally wanted to work for an ad agency, the world of Public Relations interested him just as well. Writing speeches and email campaigns for the PR firm had been brand new to Kyle when he'd started, but Jay had helped him find his footing.

By the time Kyle reached Farragut West, he'd finally talked himself into being excited about his prospects with his company's new owners. His nerves were settling. When he'd gotten dressed that morning, looking in the mirror as he'd tied his tie, he hadn't been sure if he had what it took to compete with the writers at the larger firm. He'd never been responsible for the kinds of massive campaigns they'd built, but if he could get the support—both financial and copywise—that he'd been looking for over the past few years, then he agreed with his manager that they really were about to "do some damage."

He was met in the lobby of Adoflson's building by a blond woman he'd never seen before. She was sitting with the security guards drinking out of a reusable Starbucks cup. When Kyle stepped up to the security booth and said, "Kyle Hastings here for Adolfson Partners," the blond woman spoke up.

"We're right upstairs," she said. She stepped out from behind the security booth. "I'm Marjorie Taylor," she continued, and she extended her hand for Kyle to shake. He did so, and Marjorie said, "I'm one of the junior writers with Adolfson. They sent me down here to gather up your team and bring you all up together. You're the first to arrive. Want to run out and pick up some coffee while you wait?" She finished with a tip of her cup.

Kyle shook his head. "No, thanks," he said. Marjorie was young—younger, at least, than Kyle—probably still in her early twenties. In her black pantsuit, she was quite attractive. However, Kyle's girlfriend would never approve of his desire, which he chalked up to his excitement at being at such an important firm in the middle of such an important city. He looked away from Marjorie just in time to see Todd enter the building.

When all four of Greenlight's writers were gathered together in the lobby—Jay was the last to arrive with an apology about how little parking there was in the vicinity—Marjorie led them onto the elevator and up to the fifth floor where Adolfson's offices were located.

Adolfson's office itself was spacious. The cubicles were grouped in teams, and there were a plethora of glass-enclosed meeting rooms. Outside facing windows let light in from every angle. The floor plan appeared so modern compared to Greenlight's ramshackle appearance. Kyle wondered what Adolfson's staff must have thought when they'd stepped into Greenlight's office. They must have hardly been able to quell their snickers. With its dingy walls and high cubicles, Greenlight was a joke compared to the parent company. They looked like a beleaguered cousin with respect to the rightful heir. Kyle swallowed hard as his team made their way down the hall behind Marjorie. He pulled at the stiff neck on his dress shirt and tie. He was sweating in his suit. He even thought he might be turning red.

The conference room they eventually entered was as sleek as the rest of Adolfson's offices. Light shone in through a wall of windows. The ring of tables in the center of the room was almost full to the brim with Adolfson's employees. They were the copywriters. There were at least 15—if not 20—of them. Kyle knew he was right to be nervous. Marjorie whispered to Greenlight's team to find seats wherever they could.

Kyle chose a corner at one of the tables. On either side of him were a man and a woman. They both nodded to him as he sat down. Kyle set his bag on the ground beside himself. He pulled his computer out, opened it up, and set it on the table in front of himself.

Kyle's computer looked so old and clunky next to the laptops Adolfson's staff had. Kyle realized those were probably company computers. He didn't have that luxury. Greenlight had never offered him a computer. He was using his own nearly decade-old PC. It appeared stained and worn. Kyle frowned. He didn't want to open it up to reveal the screen. He didn't know how Adolfson's employees kept their PCs so pristine.

The meeting began. Stephen White, Adolfson's Copy Chief, led. Kyle had met him before. Kyle's own manager had introduced the two of them when Stephen had first met Greenlight's management team. He was trying to get a feel for what kind of copy needs the acquired company might have, whether his own team might be of any use to them. Kyle hadn't been intimidated when he'd first met Stephen. He'd assumed they were on somewhat equal footing, but now he knew that assumption was false.

Stephen led the meeting with a clarity Kyle had never witnessed in another writer. He asked pointed questions of every other writer there. What were they working on? How could they improve their copy? What techniques would lead to better results? And if the junior writer didn't have an answer, Stephen offered them a solution.

Kyle was overwhelmed. Stephen asked his staff questions Kyle had never even considered when writing. Together, they were all working to get to the heart of the issues, to convince their prospects of the actions they needed to take. Kyle knew he and his team weren't going to be included in the meeting's specifics. Adolfson's copy team had a rhythm and flow that could only have been learned by participation. They'd been trained in their responses. They'd honed their crafts. If Kyle hadn't been so terrified, he would have been inspired.

Then, before Stephen drew the meeting to a close, he finally said, "And if you all hadn't noticed, we've had some visitors with us here today. The copy team from Greenlight Media, who we acquired last year, joined us as observers."

Kyle felt the eyes that had been trained on Stephen throughout the meeting suddenly turn to him and his three colleagues scattered throughout the room. Once again, he felt warm underneath his collar.

Stephen asked, "Now, do you all have anything we could help you with?"

The room remained silent. Kyle felt like he should say

something. The looks on his colleagues faces made him think they all might have felt the same way. But nobody from Greenlight seemed to be able to think of anything to say. With guilty expressions, they glanced across the room at one another. Stephen looked disappointed in the new team. "No?" he asked. When Greenlight's team still remained silent, he said, "Well, then, I guess that's about it." The meeting adjourned.

Kyle and the rest of Greenlight's copywriting team were back in the lobby where Marjorie had first picked them up and where—with a final smile—she'd now deposited them once again. There'd been a buffet lunch for the meeting's attendees so everyone was well fed. Although, nobody from Greenlight had really spoken since before the meeting began. "You guys want to get a drink?" Jay asked them all.

He took a final swig off his coffee cup and threw it away beside the elevator. It was only a little after noon. Todd nodded. He looked defeated. Katharine shrugged. With wide eyes, she appeared overwhelmed. "Sure," Kyle said, sensing the mood of his team.

They crossed the street and walked a half block to an Irish pub that was already open but mostly empty. They sat down at the bar. Todd and Kyle each ordered a Guiness. Jay had an IPA, and Katharine asked for a glass of red wine.

After glancing around the room and taking his first sip, Jay said, "We're going to lose our jobs."

Everybody was silent. They stared at their respective drinks. Eventually, Katharine asked, "Why do you think that?"

Jay said, "Think about what we just experienced. They've trained that team from the ground up, and they weren't making the kind of money you and I are making right now when they started. Adolfson doesn't need us. This was our chance to show them what we had to offer, and we blew it."

"What do you mean? What we had to offer?" Kyle asked his mentor.

"When Stephen told us to speak up. We each needed to say something, and we all choked. We proved to them we have nothing to offer. We can't compete," Jay said. He took another sip off his IPA.

"My manager says Adolfson wants our staff. She says we're top notch," Todd said. He was resting his chin on his arms which were crossed over the bar. He looked as young as he actually was.

"No. They don't want us," Jay said. He wiped his sleeve across his mouth. "They never wanted us. They want our clients. We're collateral. They've given us a chance to prove ourselves, and we've failed. Miserably."

With Jay's observation, the other copywriters all grew silent. Todd stared off into space. Katharine twirled her wine glass at the stem. Kyle took a sip off his Guiness. As the bitter flavor coated his throat, he asked, "So what do we do now?"

Jay shrugged. He pushed his glasses up on the bridge of his nose. "Well, aside from praying," he said, "I suggest you all do your best to kill whatever campaigns you're working on right now. Knock these ones out of the park. Get creative, and you might stand a chance. As for me, I'm going to start looking for a new job. I've been doing this long enough to know I'll never have what Adolfson's team is looking for." With drawn lips, Jay took a final swig off his IPA.

Back on the Metro on his ride home, Kyle kept thinking about what Jay had said. He needed to kill his current campaign. He needed to compete. He stared out the window at the sparks flying past in the tunnel the subway train was roaring through. A will to win rose in him, but as soon as it appeared, it was gone. Jay was his mentor. Could Kyle really be that much better than him? If the more experienced copywriter didn't think he could compete, could Kyle?

Kyle smoothed down the creases in his trousers. He narrowed his eyes. He wanted to fight, but he knew—in reality—he'd better start looking for a new job.

Sometimes You Have to Jump the Snake

It had been a dreary vacation so far. Both outside the cabin they were staying in and inside the mind he was trapped in. Two days of being trapped in a constant drizzle in the mountains of Southwest Virginia. Two days of thinking about having to apply for jobs when they returned to DC. Then, the sun gilded the windowpanes' dusty ledges as if the world itself were coming into existence for the first time. Jacob looked up from the book he'd immersed himself in. Light lingered in his unaccustomed eyes. He blinked. He said to Marigold, "Maybe we should take that walk you were talking about now."

Reading her own book with her bare feet curled beneath her on the couch, Marigold glanced up as well. She looked at the bright light refracting through the sheen on the still-damp windows. Amid the cabin's heavy silence, she too blinked to break the darkened spell. "Maybe you're right," she said. She closed her book and stood up. Jacob did the same.

Shaking off his stupor, Jacob cracked and realigned his spine as he stretched his arms and back. Marigold yawned. She smiled. Jacob smiled back at her. But the grin only stretched across his lips. It didn't reach his eyes. He finished his earlier thought. "This may be our only chance," he said. Marigold nodded. She agreed.

They each slipped out of the pajamas they'd worn since

first arriving at the cabin two days earlier. And they each slipped into jeans, tee shirts, and shoes. The shoes were for the mud. The tee shirts were for their comfort. And the jeans were to keep them safe from ticks and Lyme disease. Even with the rain, the late August heat was sure to be sweltering, infused with the kind of humidity that would turn the dense woods into steam rooms like the ones at that spa they'd visited at the National Harbor on Valentine's Day. After spraying one another with bug spray on the screened porch, Jacob and Marigold set off for the trail the cabin's owner had told them would wind through the woods and up to a vista on the hill above.

Even outside, Jacob still couldn't shake his gloom. Marigold knew that. They'd been together almost two years now. Many things they each felt were obvious to the other simply from subtle expressions and body positions. They'd recently even gotten to the point where one might know the mind of the other before the other was aware themselves. Right then wasn't one of those times, though.

"So, what's going on?" Marigold asked Jacob as they trudged up the dirt road to where their path started in earnest.

"Hm? What? Oh, nothing," Jacob said, still lost in his head even without a book mere inches from his face.

"Okay," Marigold said, not wanting to press the issue. She didn't want to risk a fight. She knew Jacob was under tremendous pressure. He had been for a while. His job had been coming to an untimely end for nearly six months. And the day before they left on that trip, he'd finally been let go. They'd been talking about moving in together since April, but Jacob had always said he wanted to be more settled in his career before they took that step. At 32 years of age, he was just starting to get his feet under him. The recent action on the part of his employer may have set their hopes back by months. If moving in together was even both of their hopes. Marigold wasn't sure.

While Jacob wasn't sure yet whether something was actually bothering him. A spate of feelings and incoherent thoughts clouded his mind. He was uncomfortable. But he couldn't pinpoint why. He scrunched up his face in an external manifestation of internal thoughts that Marigold could read somewhat clearly. But she decided not to recognize at the moment.

They reached the dirt trailhead, stepped off the gravel drive they'd been walking up, and began their hike in earnest. To the left, a decrepit, old barn was propped up against the trees slicing into the sky. In stark juxtaposition to the structure itself, a brand new red and green tractor rested idle in front of it.

In their boots, they passed through knee-high grasses on either side of the trail. A light dew settled into the cuffs of their jeans, wetting the denim so it dragged heavily against their ankles. Marigold ventured once more, "Are you sure nothing's wrong?"

Jacob stopped walking. He leaned back, breathed in deep, and finally said, "Of course something's wrong." He stopped speaking for a moment as he looked farther up the hill. Up there, the path wound around a turn. The rest of the trail was invisible. Jacob admitted, "I just don't know what it is."

It wasn't the answer she wanted to hear, but Marigold was grateful Jacob had finally acknowledged her question. They had a lot to talk about that hadn't been broached yet. Marigold cocked her head to the side, squinted her eyes, and looked at her boyfriend intently.

Jacob blurted out, "Marigold, I don't have a job when we

get back to DC, and that means anything could happen. I mean anything. You may not realize it yet, but I can't afford my apartment on what I'll get from unemployment. So, once my severance package runs out, I really don't know what I'm going to do. Worst case scenario, I might have to move back in with my mom in Massachusetts…"

"You could always move in with me," Marigold said, cutting Jacob off in mid-tirade.

Jacob gave her a sidelong glance. Marigold read that to mean, *Are you crazy? That's* never *been the plan…* With Jacob, everything had to follow a "plan." Marigold's heart shrank inside her chest, and that read visibly on her face. But Jacob simply looked over the grasses stretching out beyond them, their tips blowing in the slight breeze trotting up the hill. There were definitely ticks hidden in those grasses. Jacob wiped the back of his neck and stepped forward into the sun now blossoming over them. Marigold followed.

As he walked, Jacob kept talking, "It's not that I don't want to move in with you. It just doesn't make sense yet." Jacob bent his head forward. He looked to his left and down his nose at Marigold. He was four years older than her. She was staring at the hardened dirt packing down tighter as it retreated beneath their feet. Feeling the entire world spin around them, she sighed.

Jacob continued, "I mean, we've talked about what it takes to be ready to move in together, and we're not at that point yet." He swallowed slowly, hoping he wasn't exposing himself by revealing too much. The truth itself had to remain hidden. Even to Jacob. Discovering it was always an imminent danger. Stepping from fantasy to falsehood, reality was something better overleaped. "I'm simply afraid of moving too fast." He finished with a mumble, "You know that."

Away from the cabin they'd been confined to, away from the book she'd immersed herself in, Marigold was confronted by the obfuscation Jacob presented. She was confounded by the confusion her boyfriend had discovered. Now, Marigold was the one chasing thoughts through her mind as if she were a child trying to catch crickets in the grass beside them. It didn't make any sense.

Jacob had always sounded so sure when they'd spoken. There shouldn't have been any question. They were committed to each other completely. Or so Marigold had begun to assume. Maybe that had been her mistake. One should never assume. She cursed her own naivete. Jacob lost himself to his thoughts once again. Marigold glanced up at the path reaching onwards ahead of them.

Grasses still swayed in the distance, but the trail itself had grown steeper. The landscape had grown rockier. Pebbles imbedded themselves in the trail's mud. Suddenly, Marigold's face blanched. With a stutter-step, she stopped walking. She tugged at Jacob's arm. With a shake of his head, he stopped, too. He looked up from where his boots stuck to the ground, and he glanced ahead at where his girlfriend was pointing.

Cutting off their path, sunning itself across the width of the entire trail, a black snake lay supine along the ground. Its scales appeared slick from the mist. Like it might slip from your grip if you had the guts to catch it. It hadn't become aware of them yet. It wasn't moving. "Is it alive?" Marigold whispered.

"I think so," Jacob nodded. Although, he couldn't have known for sure.

"Do you know what kind it is?" Marigold wondered.

Jacob shook his head, *No*. "Do you?" he asked.

"No," Marigold answered. She was still whispering.

"Then, it could be poisonous," Jacob said.

Marigold nodded. "Do you think we should head back?"

Jacob was stunned into silence. A memory lay hidden beneath his conscious experience. It contained some sort of meaning to be applied to that very moment. But Jacob couldn't wrap his mind around it. The thoughts themselves took too long to comprehend. However, internal time doesn't maintain a one-to-one correspondence with external time. During the split second before he answered Marigold's question, Jacob's inner mind's eye gazed upon an entire world waiting to be uncovered behind the foreground of his senses.

* * * *

It was shortly after Jacob's parents divorced. Before he and his mom had moved back to Massachusetts. Jacob was probably about seven or eight. His grandmother and his cousin, Alex, were visiting from back east. Jacob had taken them on a walk through the trails on the hill behind their Southern California home, a route he'd often taken when his dad had still lived with them. Over his grandmother's protestations, Alex, who was four years older than Jacob and getting ready to enter middle school, had gone wandering off ahead on his own. Jacob was holding his grandmother's hand when they approached the large sandpit all the paths on those trails eventually fed straight into.

That sandpit was like the hill's ocean in that way. Everything ran into it, and that sandpit was where Jacob had really wanted to wind up in the first place. It was the whole reason he'd led his grandmother and Alex, who had completely disappeared by that point in time, on their pointless adventure. He'd wanted to pretend he was an army man in the desert. He and Alex could run and leap and land in the sand as they fought off imaginary bad guys. Alex was the best person to play army with, but Alex had disappeared.

Jacob's grandmother was shouting for his cousin to *come back, now*! From the invectives muttered under her breath, Jacob could tell she was getting angrier and angrier by the moment. Then, they heard Alex's voice way off in the distance shout, "*Hello!*" Followed by a stifled snicker.

"Alex, this isn't funny! You get back here right now!" Jacob's grandmother shouted back. Jacob looked down. He sure was glad he wasn't Alex right then. Their grandmother sounded very angry, and even Jacob was starting to get a little scared about what could potentially happen to his cousin all alone in what seemed the wilderness to Jacob. Although, his imagination was neither as vivid nor as realistic as his grandmother's. Jacob looked up and forward once again.

That was when he saw it. Stretched across the steps leading up to the sandpit, a snake was sunning itself in the afternoon light. Its scales appeared slick beneath the glare. At a glance, Jacob was certain it was a rattlesnake (although, he couldn't have known for sure). That's how he always remembered the story. That a rattlesnake had cut off his and his grandmother's ascent to the sandpit. That a rattlesnake had taught him the truth of what had always lain hidden around every corner of those trails he'd walked so carefree along with his dad when the older man had still lived with them.

Jacob screamed and tugged at his grandmother's hand. He pointed straight ahead of them.

"Goodness!" his grandmother exclaimed as she noticed the snake and stopped mid-step while frantically looking in every direction. Presumably with the hope of discovering her other grandson, Alex, to be safe as well. Confronted by that clear and present danger, though, her heart must have been in her throat.

When Alex suddenly reappeared to their left. In a blur, he sped past Jacob and their grandmother. He looked over his right shoulder as he reached the base of the steps where the rattlesnake lay. "Alex!" Jacob's grandmother screamed. While Jacob himself could have sworn his cousin smiled at them as he leapt off the ground to fly overtop both the snake and all three steps like he was an Olympic long jumper. With a slight bend to his knees, Alex landed safely in the sandpit. A puff of dust settled around him.

"Alex! What are you thinking?" their grandmother screamed. Alex shrugged. "How do you expect to get back from there now?" she continued nearly apoplectic. Alex shrugged once more. With a sudden run and another puff of dust, he lifted off into another leap and joined them at the base of the steps. That time, Jacob was certain. A smile lifted his cousin's lips.

Their grandmother grabbed Alex by the arm. He might have been larger than Jacob, but he was smaller than her. She dragged Alex down the hill at quite a clip, admonishing him the whole way for going off on his own, asking him if he understood the dangers he might have faced. Boy, was he going to be in trouble when they got home, she told him. But Alex kept on smiling over his shoulder at Jacob following slightly behind, trying hard to keep up in case another snake was waiting right beside the path to bite him on the heel.

As far as Jacob knew, his grandmother never revealed what had happened on the hill to another grown up. How she had lost control. And it was never discussed by the three of them again. But later that night, when from the bottom bunk, the younger of the two whispered to ask his elder cousin what had ever possessed him to make that fortuitous leap, Alex responded quite simply, "Sometimes, you have to jump the snake."

* * * *

"No. I don't think we should go back," Jacob said with uncharacteristic force. Marigold's eyes widened. She had been almost certain the man she had come to know over the past couple years would want to return to the safety of the cabin and their books in the face of such an unexpected turn of events. She looked at Jacob. "Sometimes, you have to jump the snake," he told her. Even though, he didn't know why. "Who should go first?"

Marigold wasn't sure. "Maybe we should go together," she said.

Jacob nodded. He and Marigold held hands. They walked up the path slowly until they were a short distance away from the snake. Then, with a nod at one another and a couple quick steps, they leaped into the air and overtop the snake. When they landed, their hearts racing, they looked back over their shoulders at the danger passed. The snake didn't care. It hadn't bothered to look at them or even to slither away. Marigold laughed. Jacob joined her. "I guess we need to keep our eyes open," Jacob admitted. With a nod, Marigold agreed.

As they continued their trek up the muddy, dirt-packed hill, Jacob finally admitted, "The truth is I'm scared, Marigold. I don't know if I'll find a job in DC, and I don't know how long I can keep looking only here. There aren't a lot of agencies in the District. I may have to go back to New York, or up to Boston, or else out to God knows where if we're not ready to move in together yet…"

Marigold was nodding along as if she understood. But suddenly, she stopped. She let go of her boyfriend's hand as they walked. Her palm had grown a little too sweaty. Jacob didn't notice. He'd been too busy talking. As far as Marigold was concerned, they might not have been together forever yet, but they'd been together long enough. A job shouldn't drive them apart at that point. All Jacob needed was to make a commitment. Like she had. To the city, to a career, to their relationship. Marigold hung her head. Maybe the truth he'd been hiding was that, even at 32, he simply wasn't ready. Quite uncharacteristically, Marigold said, "You need to make up your mind, then. Because when you say *we're* not ready, it sounds more like you're saying *you're* not ready…"

Jacob was taken aback. Usually, Marigold hedged her words around his feelings. He looked down. A surge of emotions slithered around inside of him.

Marigold was still talking, "I mean, you haven't even given it a shot yet. You haven't applied to a single job, and you're already talking about leaving DC. That makes me feel like maybe you never intended to stay here in the first place. Maybe you never thought we'd be together this long at all. Maybe you *never* planned on us moving in together, which by the way, is precisely why people date in the first place. To get to *this* place. Maybe you just don't know what real love is."

Jacob glanced over at his girlfriend. He didn't want to believe her. He knew what real love was. Or so he believed.

They continued in silence once again. For different reasons than they'd walked in silence earlier. Marigold was replaying everything she'd said in her head. Jacob was containing his anger at his girlfriend's accusations. Despite what they each believed, honesty had never been the cornerstone of their relationship. It's rarely the cornerstone of any relationship. Although, neither of them had ever been aware of that before. It's difficult to first bear witness to the decay attached to your cherished institutions. It makes the entire world appear to be rotting away like an old barn with a brand-new tractor out front.

Then, they reached the vista at the apex of the hike. It formed a flat, grassy plateau. All of Virginia stretched out before them. The state spread out around them. They could probably see all the way to North Carolina from there. Mountains and hills rose and descended far into the distance. Their green and brown pastures added splotches of color to the monochromatic skies. A blue-gray cloud hung over them. Rain still fell in sheets in the distance. It surrounded the two of them atop that hill. But alone together, they remained dry.

Marigold walked across the plateau to the hill's edge. Like a figurehead protruding from the bow of a ship, she stood there as if she were ready to leap. Jacob walked up behind her. She heard him, but she didn't notice him. A lone bull stared back at them from a hill across the way. Jacob could see the bull presumably chewing his cud. Cows and calves were paddocked farther down that same hill. From the distance, the entire bovine family was little more than a set of miniature pieces. They were like the plastic toys from Jacob's childhood. *How lonely*, Jacob thought as he contemplated that bull alone in his pen. Without saying another word, he wrapped his arms around Marigold. Instead of leaping, she leaned back into him. Jacob suddenly realized what it meant for them to jump that snake.

Thank You So Much for Coming

For the first time ever, they'd been confronted with the question of what gift they should bring an extended family member who wanted nothing to do with them. That much had been made clear. Their political opinions were detestable to that branch of the family, deranged and malignant ideas that would only lead to distress and dissolution for the nation. After eliminating all the items from the registry, they settled on a handmade gift they picked out themselves—a series of photographs of mundane objects (a metal beam, the railing of a park bench, etc.) mounted on a single canvas that spelled out the groom's last name: Isaac.

At the time of their niece's birth in 1993, they were already in their forties. Mary, the wife, was a decade older than her sister, Annie. And by the time Annie's daughter, Dawn, married Charlie Isaac in 2018, Mary and her husband were both retired and living on fixed incomes. Unlike her sister, Mary had refused to vote for Hillary Clinton, which Annie had said was the last straw in their relationship. She cut Mary and her husband, Joe, out of her life for good. Mary and Joe, however, had never had children of their own. Annie's two kids were the closest things they had to living descendants, and since Donald Trump had been sworn in as the 45th president of the United States, they hadn't heard a word from that branch of the family until the wedding invitation showed up six months earlier.

That Saturday, though, the day of the wedding, everything had gone right. They'd left their home in

Waynesboro, VA early that morning for the three hour-long drive up to Alexandria where the wedding was being held that afternoon. They'd decided not to stay at a hotel the night before since they still weren't sure if they were actually invited. Although they'd received the invitation and RSVP'd, they never heard a word from any of their family members confirming it. Mary and Annie's parents had both passed away. Their father at a relatively young age in the late 1990s and their mother at an older age in the mid-2010s when Obama was still president.

At the ceremony, they'd waited patiently in their seats for Annie to be brought in by her son, James. With the rest of their extended family living out West, neither Mary nor Joe knew anybody else there. Mary hid her gaze as her sister walked down the aisle with her escort. She'd never met Charlie, the young man standing at the head of the ceremony, before. But her eyes brimmed with tears as she saw Dawn, her only niece, behind a veil, enter the building with Annie's ex-husband, Bill.

The ceremony didn't last long. Mary dabbed her eyes through the entire exchange. Joe held her hand. The officiant was a woman, and the venue wasn't a church. But it was the most beautiful thing Mary had witnessed since she'd stood at the top of her own aisle many years before and gazed into Joe's eyes. As she glanced around at the other attendants, some of their faces even began to appear familiar to her. In the midst of her emotion, it was as if she had been with those people her whole life. Although, she knew hardly anything of her sister's and niece's lives in Northern Virginia.

The last time she and Joe had been up to Alexandria to visit that branch of the family had been before Obama had been elected, when Mary admitted to her sister that she and Joe had voted for Hillary Clinton in the primary because she feared what an Obama presidency might do to the United

States. "So instead of voting in the Republican primary, you two wasted your votes simply to make sure a black man wouldn't become our president?" Annie said. After that, Mary and Annie traded a few more words, and the younger sister never invited her older sister or her brother-in-law to come visit her family in Northern Virginia ever again.

That had been nearly a decade earlier, and although Mary tried reaching out to her sister, she was more often than not rebuffed. But long before the final schism, she and her husband had feared their days as a coherent family were numbered. Their politics had become too divisive. Even during the Bush years, Joe had stormed out of Annie's house on more than one occasion in a rage culminating with, "Get in the car, Mary. We're leaving." He couldn't accept the liberal politics of the Northern Virginia branch, and they couldn't accept Joe and Mary's conservatism. Neither Joe nor Mary considered themselves radical. Joe had attended a few Tea Party rallies at the beginning of Obama's presidency, but James was the one who had practically camped out with Occupy Wall Street at the end of the 44th president's second term. It seemed like everything that was said between the two branches had a deeper meaning. Mary thought Joe's words were often taken out of context, and she could see behind what Annie was feigning to what her sister really believed. It could have been pure paranoia, but the gap widened. Mary thought Annie was overreacting. However, before long, they couldn't find any common ground.

Things hadn't always been that way, though. Annie had looked up to her older sister when she'd been in college protesting the Vietnam War, and Mary had smoked pot with Annie when she'd visited the younger girl on her own college campus at the start of her career. But things change over a forty-year period. Our memories fade, and we see the past through the lens of the present. Neither Mary nor Annie believed they were much different than they'd been back when Mary was practically raising Annie while she worked her way through high school, but they were. There was no way they couldn't be. They'd had their own individual experiences in their own individual places. And although they'd started at similar points, they'd moved in opposite directions.

When the ceremony ended, Mary could barely contain her joy… or her trepidation. She wanted to run away before the reception. She wanted to enjoy her fantasy of family connection, and she was afraid reality would intrude if she were forced to interact with her family for any actual amount of time. Only Joe kept her there. He refused to get the car. "We need to stay for dinner," he said. "Besides, Bill probably already paid for our meal. It would be rude to leave now." He remembered those kinds of details from their own wedding almost forty years earlier. Mary smiled at her husband. She was frightened, but she agreed.

Silently, they left the building where the ceremony was held and approached the outdoor tent where the reception would be. The grounds were beautiful. There was a river winding through the trees in the distance. Mary had never known such a gorgeous enclave existed so close to the city. Without saying a word, Mary and Joe looked for their place card. Secretly, Mary was afraid it wouldn't be there. On some level, she believed the entire day had been a mistake. But there were their names written in calligraphy on a card, with a table number beside them. Mary and Joe made their way across what might eventually become a dance floor to the seats where they could eat their fish and steak respectively.

When Joe got up to get them their drinks, Mary remained seated at the table. Across the dance floor, her sister sat at a table with her ex-husband. James was sitting between them. They were all smiling at the sweetheart table at the head of the tent where Dawn and Charlie would soon be seated. Seeing the three of them there like they were still a family themselves, Mary remembered so much of her life. She thought back to when her younger sister had been born. She remembered quite clearly holding the little girl as a baby at the hospital where her mother had given birth. She remembered the first time she'd heard Annie say a word she could comprehend. And she remembered when she'd said goodbye to her baby sister on the day she headed off for college. Then, a swell of recorded jazz blasted out of the speakers, and the DJ proclaimed, "May I introduce you all for the first time to Mr. and Mrs. Charles Isaac!" Along with the rest of the wedding, Mary erupted in thunderous cheering and applause.

All this and much more Mary remembered while Joe was away gathering their drinks. She remembered the joy she'd felt when her sister had given birth to Dawn and later to James. She and her husband had invited their niece and nephew down from DC on many occasions during the summer. And as children in the late 1990s and early 2000s, they'd always gone. Annie and Bill had appreciated their time together alone, or so Mary had always believed prior to the couple's divorce in 2010. It wasn't that Mary and Joe had never wanted children. They were simply incapable. In the 21st century, medicine might have been able to overcome their problems, but when Mary had still been fertile, science hadn't advanced quite so far yet. Mary frowned.

It was nearly 9:00 when Mary felt a tap on her shoulder. She turned from the conversation she was having with one of the other couples at their table. She'd been nervous to talk to anybody. She didn't know how to handle her estrangement. But the other couples at the table never asked anything that might even force her to admit that fact. Not only that, but Joe had discovered he and one of the other guys saw eye-to-eye politically. They weren't exactly fans of Trump, but they were thrilled the Democrats had finally lost power. Mary looked up.

With Charlie at her side, Dawn was smiling at her. The girl was glowing so beautifully. "Hello, Aunt Mary," she said. "Thank you so much for coming."

More tears welled behind Mary's eyes than had been there even when her niece was saying her vows. "Thank you so much for inviting us, Dawn," she said.

"Oh, mom wouldn't have let me do this if you weren't here," Dawn said. She laughed, and she and her new husband moved around to their right to greet the other couples at the table.

"Did you hear that?" Mary whispered to Joe. "She said Annie wanted me here."

Joe smiled. He hadn't heard, but he put his arm around his wife. He hugged her close.

"Maybe I should go say something to her," Mary said.

"To Annie?" Joe asked.

Mary nodded. Her husband tensed in his seat. He didn't want to discourage his wife from speaking with her sister, but given the many times she'd tried reaching out to her and been refused, he wasn't sure. But it was their niece's wedding after all. Annie wouldn't have invited them if she hadn't expected them to say something to her. "Maybe you should," Joe finally said.

"All right," Mary said. "Once we finish our drinks, I'm going to go say hi." *That way if she still despises me*, Mary thought, *we'll have no reason to stay.*

Even though he was still apprehensive, Joe smiled at his wife. "Sounds good," he said, and he returned to the conversation he was having with his fellow Republican.

Standing up after her drink was done, Mary smoothed down her dress. She prayed she still looked as presentable as she'd hoped she'd looked when the day had first started. She hadn't seen her family in over two years, and there had already been a long drive, an entire ceremony to sit through, a meal and two drinks, not to mention the overwhelming emotions of the day. Mary held her head high, and she took a step toward the table where her sister was still seated looking in the opposite direction at another guest with whom she was speaking. Mary didn't hear her husband say, "Good luck," as she walked away.

She reached Annie's table. With a smile at the guest to whom Annie was speaking with, Mary sat down. The other guest nodded at her and stepped away. Annie turned in her seat to face her sister for the first time in a long while.

"Hi, Annie," Mary said.

Annie smiled. "Hi, Mary," she said.

"How are you?" Mary asked.

"I'm good," Annie said. "And you?"

Mary started trembling. She wanted to tell her sister it had been hell living without her for nearly two years. She wanted to tell her she was so grateful to be invited to the wedding and simultaneously so angry that she'd never met her niece's fiancé. But she forced a smile and said, "I'm good, too."

Annie leaned across a vacant chair between them. She embraced her sister. "It's so good to see you," she said.

Mary felt a lump of tears move into her throat. She wanted to heave with a sob, but she didn't feel safe enough to reveal her emotions yet. "It's good to see you, too," she managed to mumble as she returned Annie's embrace.

The two sisters let one another go. They sat in silence together for a few more minutes. Then, Mary stood up. "Well, I'm sure you have other guests you need to attend to," she said.

"I do," Annie said with a smile.

Mary nodded. She turned around to return to her table. Joe was sitting there patiently, watching the interaction between the two sisters. He, too, looked like he had tears in his eyes. As Mary took her first step away from her sister, she heard Annie say, "Thank you so much for coming, Mary."

Maybe the Afterlife Is Our Real Life

They hadn't seen one another in a while. It was through no fault of their own. Too much had been going on. Stuart and his wife, Alison, were in their car on the way over to visit Gabe and Erin who lived in Southeast DC with their newborn baby girl, Shay. Stuart and Alison hadn't met Shay yet. She was already three months old. The two couples were close. Stuart and Gabe had been friends for a few years, but the two couples hadn't had a chance to get together since they'd gone out for brunch in May. Erin's pregnancy had been almost full-term by then. Now, it was a rainy Tuesday night at the end of September.

"We've been through so much since then," Stuart said in reference to the last time they'd seen Gabe and Erin. "I guess they've been through a lot, too," he added. He frowned. Alison reached over and grabbed Stuart's right hand from where it rested on the gear shift between the seats. She squeezed his palm. Stuart glanced back at her. His eyes appeared wounded, but he smiled at his wife just the same. She smiled back at him with a similar expression.

They pulled up and parked across the street from the gate to Gabe and Erin's condo development. That gate was never closed. It was never locked. Stuart didn't know what purpose it served. The development their friends lived in was new. It wasn't as new as the apartment building Stuart and Alison shared in Petworth in Northwest, but Gabe and Erin's development had been built in historic Anacostia less than five years earlier. Gabe was one of the first people to move into it shortly before he started dating Erin. It was the best deal he believed he could find in the District back then. It was an investment.

Gabe answered the door before they even knocked. He must have been on the lookout for them. That might have been because as they stepped into their friends' condo, Stuart and Alison saw the newborn baby girl, Shay, asleep in her mother's arms. Stuart blinked. With her fat cheeks and pudgy fingers, Shay resembled a Renaissance cherub. "I didn't want to wake the baby," Gabe whispered. Stuart and Alison each nodded knowingly. Although, neither of them actually had any idea.

"Can I get you guys anything to drink?" Gabe asked. Stuart had a beer. Alison asked for a La Croix. She joined Erin on the couch where the mother was sitting with the baby in her arms. Even though she was asleep, Shay's mouth and lips kept moving like she was breastfeeding. She needed her mother. Gabe invited Stuart out onto the porch off the kitchen where the two of them could talk more animatedly without disturbing Shay.

Once they were outside, Gabe asked, "So, how have you been?"

Stuart shrugged. "We've been good." He sighed. "But you know, we've been trying to get pregnant, and we've run into some difficulties."

Gabe's expression turned from joyful to serious. "What kind of difficulties?" he asked.

Stuart said, "Well, it's been over a year now, and it just hasn't been happening. So, finally, over the summer, Alison suggested we have some tests run. It turns out she has PCOS. That stands for Polycystic Ovarian Syndrome. As a result, she doesn't ovulate quite right. We really want to have a baby, but it isn't going to be possible without help."

Stuart looked defeated. He said, "I don't want to drag you down with everything you guys have been going through lately, but it's been hard on us. Alison really wants to be a mom, and I really want to be a dad. But right now, we don't know if that's possible."

Gabe took a sip off his own beer. "I don't think that's really a big deal," he said. "They can do so much now for people in your position. It's not like back when our parents were trying to get pregnant. I don't think you'll have any trouble having a baby. It just might take a little work, but anything worth having is worth working for, am I right?"

Gabe smiled. Stuart smiled back at him. Everybody had said that to him—his friends, his parents, even the doctors. It was nothing new for him to hear, but the sentiment always relieved his anxiety. "You're right," Stuart said. Then, he added, "So, how have you guys been?"

It was Gabe's turn to frown. Stuart could tell his friend wanted to pretend like everything had been going as great as it should have been, but his eyes couldn't lie. He said, "Well, having Shay has been out of this world. In just a few months, she's already brought so much joy to my life. I never knew—and I certainly never believed—how amazing having a baby could be. But, you know, with everything with my mom. It just…"

Gabe's voice trailed off as he looked away at the construction occurring on the other side of the fence from his condo development. Stuart followed Gabe's gaze with his own. The old building across from them was being demolished and rebuilt into something brand new. Stuart wondered what sort of events had occurred in that building when it had housed people. He wondered what sort of events had occurred in that building since it had been abandoned.

"I was so sorry to hear about that," Stuart interjected. He'd seen how Gabe's mom had passed away a couple weeks after Shay had been born. Those two major life events were the reason he and Alison had given Gabe and Erin such a wide berth over the past few months. Neither of them knew what the appropriate amount of time was for mourning the death of a parent or for getting settled in with a newborn. But right then, Stuart wanted to hear what his friend had been through and what he'd discovered. "How are you handling it?"

Gabe inhaled deeply. He said, "It's hard, you know. Losing a parent is hard. And my dad's sick now, too."

"Oh, man, I'm so sorry to hear that."

"Yeah, we're probably going to lose him in the next couple months as well."

"That's terrible. What's wrong with him?"

"It's his heart," Gabe said. "It happened right after my mom went into hospice for the cancer. My dad collapsed the next day. I took him to the hospital, and they said his heart was giving out. He's probably never even going to meet his granddaughter." Gabe's gaze grew distant as he stared at the construction site across from them. It was as if he were seeing something that existed behind the building's physicality. He said, "The doctors told us he could probably survive it if he wanted to, but he doesn't. Not without my mom. It's like he's dying of a broken heart."

Stuart glanced back at the window through the kitchen to the living room on the other side. His own wife, Alison, played there with Gabe and Erin's newborn baby girl who was awake now. The sight of his wife playing with that child brought warmth to Stuart's heart. "That's really sad," he said.

"Yeah, I know," Gabe said. "My mom would want

him to live. She was so full of life, and she loved him so much, but he's giving up. He doesn't want to be here anymore. That's what he says."

Stuart bowed his head. He wondered if he would still want to live if his own wife passed away. He asked, "How long were they married?"

"Thirty-five years," Gabe said.

"That's a long time." Stuart had only been married to Alison for two years, and he already couldn't imagine life without her. Even if they never were able to have children, he couldn't imagine life without her. To lose her after 25 years was unfathomable. The thought of the pain Gabe's dad must have been living through right then made Stuart want to cry.

"It was pretty surreal, though," Gabe said. Startled out of his own ruminations, Stuart turned away from the kitchen window and looked directly at his friend for the first time since they'd really started talking. "Going down to Florida to be with my mom at the end of her life right after I watched Erin give birth to Shay, that is."

"I can only imagine," Stuart said.

"I mean, Erin wasn't too happy I was leaving, but I had to go. And leaving this little cocoon of life for the reality of death was so weird. When I got to Florida, it was complete culture shock. I was so sleep deprived. Shay had only been born two days before. Part of me wanted to come right back up here to be with her and Erin, and part of me couldn't believe we were bringing life into a world where everything dies. But being with my mom at that point on her journey was so beautiful."

"I've heard that from people before when they've stayed with someone who was dying…"

Gabe's gaze grew even more distant. He said, "I held my mom's hand as she died. Her breath kept getting more ragged. Then, it all came out in one long note. It sounded like her soul was stuck in her throat. Then, it disappeared, and she was gone. I knew it as soon as it happened." Gabe took a sip off his beer. Stuart took a sip off his as well.

Gabe said, "You know, it's easy to leave this world, but it's a lot harder to enter it. I was so scared for Erin the whole time she was giving birth to Shay. The midwives kept saying everything was fine, but I didn't know. Shay came out, and then, all I saw was blood. Erin had a postpartum hemorrhage. They said they didn't need to call in a doctor. They could fix it themselves, but I didn't know…"

Gabe shook his head. Stuart swallowed slowly. Now, he was fearful of his own desire for Alison to get pregnant. There was a lot he didn't understand about the world.

"While my mom was in hospice, though," Gabe said, "I'd go swimming in her pool every evening right before it got dark. It was fresh and cleansing as if I were being born again at the end of each day. I kept thinking about how life and death were coming together in my life right at that moment."

Stuart nodded. Of course, he had never experienced what his friend was talking about. He could only imagine.

"I found myself wondering…" Gabe said, "The whole time Shay was inside Erin, she had no idea what was waiting for her on the other side. The day she was born must have been terrifying. Her entire world was collapsing in on her. With every contraction, she was being forced out into a place she never knew existed. Sure, she'd had hints of this world. She'd heard voices talking to her from the other side. She'd heard my voice even, but she didn't know all this was here. She didn't know who or what I was. I was only a *sensation*.

"I kept wondering. Is that what death is? Are we afraid of it only because we don't know what's on the other side? It could be a whole other world like this one. I mean, I definitely have *sensations* there might be something else. Maybe, we're all living in some magnificent creature's womb, and death is only another birth. Maybe the afterlife is our real life."

Stuart didn't know what to say. It wasn't an unfamiliar theory, but he'd never thought about it quite like that. Somehow, Gabe's metaphor seemed more compelling than any argument he'd heard about the afterlife before. Stuart was an atheist. Gabe was, too. They'd discussed their unbelief on many occasions. Stuart inhaled. He looked at that abandoned building across from them. He narrowed his eyes. He wondered what was going to replace it.

Moonshadow

Perhaps it was only by chance she was listening to Cat Stevens as she walked home that day. But shortly after she rounded the corner off Sherman Ave and onto Georgia Ave, she noticed a gray and white cat with a little pink nose sitting in the flowerbed of a building at the corner on Quincy. The cat was staring at her. She didn't know cats all that well. She was allergic to them, but she loved them anyway. Recently, she'd become obsessed with pictures of kittens on Facebook, and she'd been enamored by videos of newborn cats on YouTube. This particular cat had long legs but appeared malnourished. Although, since she wasn't on friendly terms with many cats since she was allergic to them, she wasn't certain of that. She lived between Quincy and Randolph. So, she was only a half a block away from home. She took the earbuds out of her ears, and she stopped for a moment to pay attention to the cat sitting still in the flowerbed.

She squatted down to get closer to eye level with the cat. She said, "Hello there. How are you today?"

The cat meowed and stepped closer to her. She hadn't expected that. Since she was allergic to cats, she stood up straight and started walking once again, leaving the cat behind. But the cat walked up to the wooden edge of the flowerbed and walked along beside her, meowing the whole time. When the two of them got to the corner of her own building, she expected the cat to return to the flowerbed, but it didn't. As the flowerbed's wooden edge came to an end, the cat hopped off the ledge and walked along on the sidewalk beside her. "Are you following me?" she asked the cat, half expecting the cat to run away at the sound of her voice. But the cat didn't run. Instead, the cat kept walking along beside her, meowing the whole time.

A woman walking past her asked, "Is that your cat?"

She laughed, "No. It just started following me."

"Well, it looks like it's your cat now," the woman said.

She smiled. She didn't believe the woman. She hummed the song she'd been listening to when she'd bumped into the cat.

When she got to the chorus, she turned to the cat and asked it, "Could that be your name? Moonshadow? Like the Cat Stevens song?" Again, she expected the cat to run away at the sound of her voice, but the cat didn't run. Instead, it kept walking along right beside her, meowing the whole time, until she got to the door of her building.

"Well, this is where I live," she said to the cat as if the cat knew it might be time to head home as soon as she used her key fob to open the building's door, as if the cat were a date who would suddenly realize he had overstayed his welcome. But the cat didn't leave. Instead, the cat stopped with her at the door, and with another meow, the cat followed at her heel as she stepped into her building's lobby.

"I didn't know you had a cat," the desk clerk said to her as she entered.

She knew the desk clerk by name. His name was Roland. She laughed and said to him, "I don't have a cat. This one just followed me home."

"Well, you might have a cat now," Roland laughed.

That's when she started getting a little nervous. She looked down at the cat. The cat appeared confused. It panicked. It started darting every which way through the building's lobby. But when she opened the door for it to go back outside, the cat wouldn't go.

"Let me help you get him on the elevator," Roland said. "You can take him to the SPCA tomorrow to see if he's microchipped so they can find his owner... if he has an owner."

Even though she was allergic to cats, she nodded. It was getting cold outside, and there was talk of snow that night. She wanted to make sure the cat was safe in her apartment, that it wouldn't freeze to death outside. She'd have to call her fiancé to make sure he was okay with the cat staying with them until they found its owner, but she would do that later. She said to the desk clerk, "That would be great."

Together, they herded the cat into the elevator. The desk clerk blocked the cat's escape with his feet, and she held the elevator door open until the cat followed her on. When she and the cat got to her floor, once again, the cat walked right along beside her, meowing the whole way until they got to her apartment. She opened the door to her fiancé's and her apartment. The cat walked in ahead of her and hopped up on the couch as if it had always lived with her. The cat fell immediately asleep

She shut the door. She didn't know what to do. The cat might have fleas. It might have a disease. She thought of everything a cat might need. She made a quick list—litter box, litter, and food. Leaving the cat alone in her apartment, she ran back downstairs to the Metro that was one block away. She took the green line one stop south of there. She ran into the Petco in Columbia Heights and bought everything she needed.

When she got back to her fiancé's and her apartment, the cat was still asleep in the same spot on the couch where it had been when she'd left. She put some food on a plate and set up the litter box in front of the bathroom. There wasn't really anywhere else to put it in their 700 square foot apartment. Then, she sat down to wait for her fiancé to call her when he was on his way home from work. She wasn't going to do anything else about the cat right then.

When her fiancé finally did call around 5:30, she said to him, "Steven, you'll never believe what happened to me today…" And she proceeded to tell him the entire story about how the cat had followed her home. She expected him to say something like—*What? Are you crazy? You're allergic to cats…*

But instead, he sighed, and he said, "Well, Lily, it sounds like he chose you."

* * * *

When Steven got home, the cat wouldn't move from its position on the couch to make space for Lily's fiancé. The cat stared at Steven as if Steven had invaded the cat's space, as if the cat had always lived in that apartment with Lily and Steven were the newcomer. "Well, I guess from the cat's perspective that's exactly how it is," Steven said to Lily. "As far as the cat knows, it was here before me."

The next morning, Lily saw that it had snowed the night before. It was only a light dusting, but she realized she might have saved the cat's life. She took the cat to the SPCA. She was hoping they would tell her it appeared to be a stray and she could keep it. But the lady at the SPCA already knew the cat. "Why, it's Cappers. Hi there, Cappers," the lady said once she scanned Cappers' microchip. "I thought it was you, boy," she said to the cat while rubbing his chin.

"Cappers first showed up here, oh, it must have been about seven or eight months ago, last September," the woman from the SPCA explained to Lily. "He was in really bad shape then, even skinnier than he is now, with an infected gash on his back and mites all over his body. Poor little guy, but he was already neutered, and we had no record of him. So, he must have had a family somewhere sometime. He stayed with us for about six months. He's the sweetest little guy. Yes, he is…" At the next sentence, Lily's stomach dropped. "A family adopted him about a month ago."

Lily frowned. "So, I won't be able to keep him," she said. In less than a day, she'd already grown quite attached to the cat. In fact, she hadn't told Steven yet, but she already knew his name. It was exactly what the cat had told her it was—Moonshadow.

"No. You'll probably be able to keep him," the woman said. "We'll call the family that adopted him, but I wouldn't be surprised if we don't hear back from them. It happens all the time."

Lily was surprised. She didn't understand why somebody would adopt a cat only to let him go less than a month later. Even a cat that had already been in the shelter system for six months. They didn't even bring him back to the SPCA where he could find another home. They simply let him go in the middle of the city where any manner of things could have happened to him. He could have frozen to death last night. Lily felt like she might cry for little Moonshadow who, right then, was rubbing his cheek against her fingers. He really was a sweet cat. "Should I take him to the vet?" Lily asked. "Because I was thinking maybe I should…"

"That wouldn't be a bad idea," the woman said. "We'll let you know if we hear anything from the family that adopted him. But according to his records and where you say you live, he was already over a mile and a half away from their home. So, who knows…"

Lily left the SPCA after the woman left a message for Cappers' new owners. She took the cat directly to a veterinarian that a friend of hers took her own cat to up in

Tenleytown. It was the only vet she knew about in the District. The woman at the SPCA had said if they didn't hear back from the new family within five days, Lily could officially adopt him. But she wasn't planning to start calling Cappers by his new name until she knew she could keep him.

However, when she got to the vet's office up in Tenleytown and they asked for the patient's name, Lily couldn't resist. "Moonshadow," she said, and she told everybody—the receptionist, the nurse, even the veterinarian herself—the story of how they'd discovered one another.

The vet assumed Moonshadow was between 10 and 12 years old, which was older than Lily had hoped he'd be. But that was okay. She'd heard about cats living all the way into their twenties before. If that other family didn't come back to claim him, she and Moonshadow could have a nice, long life together.

Other than bad teeth and gums, the only thing the vet noticed Moonshadow had wrong with him was arthritis in his back hips. It probably made his joints ache when he jumped up and down off the furniture. It might be nice for Lily and Steven to buy him some kitty steps, the vet said. However, the vet also wanted to run some lab work. Moonshadow was an older cat, the vet reminded Lily, and there could be any number of illnesses potentially causing the bad teeth and gums. The vet took blood and urine from Moonshadow, and then Lily took him home.

The next day, Lily got a call from the vet. The vet told her Moonshadow was FIV positive. "FIV is an autoimmune disorder in cats similar to HIV in humans," the vet told her. Moonshadow might have been born with it, or he could have contracted it in a street fight with another cat who was already positive. Either way, it was probably what was causing Moonshadow's dental problems, the vet added. She wanted to get a kitty cardiologist to check Moonshadow's heart, and then, they could pull the teeth causing him the most discomfort. If Lily believed that was necessary, of course. "Many cats can still live long lives with FIV, though. You just need to keep him away from other cats and watch out for him being outside. You don't want him to get sick. His body may not be able to fight off other illnesses many cats live with just fine." The vet continued, "However, Moonshadow also has stage III kidney disease."

"What does that mean?" Lily asked.

"It means his kidneys are failing him. At maximum, Moonshadow has only a few years to live." The vet continued, "It takes a special person to care for a cat at this stage of their life. I hope you understand how important you could be to him, but of course, you shouldn't feel obligated to care for him either. You could always take him back to the SPCA."

When Lily got off the phone with the vet, she gave Moonshadow a hug. She called Steven at work. She started crying as she told him what the vet had said. "But I hope we can still keep him, Steven. He really needs us. He's not in any kind of shape to be out on the streets, and he probably had a family once upon a time. He might still miss them…"

Steven agreed. Moonshadow needed them. If the current owners didn't come back to claim him, he and Lily would keep Moonshadow for as long as they could. He believed, at the very least, they might be able to make his golden years as pleasant as possible.

* * * *

Nobody ever claimed Moonshadow from the SPCA. Lily officially adopted him five days after they'd met one another that afternoon when she was walking home. She took him back to the vet, and the vet made recommendations for two medications she and Steven should put Moonshadow on immediately. One was a liquid for his arthritis. The other was a pill for his kidney disease. Every night, they had to squirt the liquid into his mouth and shove the pill down his throat.

Moonshadow didn't struggle much when they gave him his medications. Lily was impressed. However, a week or two after they started giving the medications to him, when Lily was cleaning up their bedroom, she found a number of Moonshadow's pills stuffed under the corner of the comforter for their bed. Apparently, most nights, just like with any 10 to 12-year-old human child who doesn't want to take the medicines he's being given, Moonshadow would fake swallowing the pills, spit them out, and shove them under the comforter where he hoped they'd never be found.

"Oh, Moonshadow," Lily said, "you're too smart for your own good."

In the morning, Moonshadow walked up onto Lily's chest and lay there purring. She woke up and stared at him staring back at her. She scratched him under the chin. Moonshadow blinked at her. Then, once Lily was fully awake, Moonshadow climbed down and tapped Steven on the shoulder. It was as if the cat were saying, *Excuse me, sir, I need you for a moment.* But it wasn't because Moonshadow needed to be fed. Lily and Steven free fed him, and he never overate. It was simply because he liked cuddling with both of them before they started their days. Once they were both awake, Moonshadow walked back and forth from one to the other, rubbing his cheek against their hands, purring, licking their fingers, and giving them both soft little headbutts, which, Lily discovered via the internet, was a great sign of affection from a cat.

"I think Moonshadow grew up with a family that had a dog," Lily said to Steven.

"Why do you think that?" Steven asked.

"Because he always licks us. You know, that's not a normal sign of affection from a cat, but he could have learned it from a dog if he grew up with one…"

Steven nodded.

"I wish I knew how he grew up," Lily said. "I wish I'd known his previous family. Maybe they had kids. Maybe his best friend *was* a dog. If they're still around, I wish I could bring him back to them. I love him so much, but if he loves another family, I want him to be with them."

"I think Moonshadow is very happy with us," Steven said. "He always seems so grateful that we found him."

"I hope so," Lily said, "but I don't know. He had a home somewhere else once upon a time. If he wanted to be with that family instead of us, I'd gladly let him go back to them if it would make him happy."

In the afternoon, Moonshadow stared back at Lily from the sliding glass door leading onto the small balcony off their apartment. From where she sat on the couch doing her work and watching television, she smiled at the cat. "Okay, Moonshadow," she said.

Lily stood up. She walked over to the door, and she opened it for Moonshadow. He stepped out into the sunlight streaming across their tiny balcony. He licked the low-lying herbs Lily grew out there, and he lay down in the light. He stretched his long body across the balcony, and he flicked his tail until he got comfortable.

After a while, Moonshadow stood back up and—similar to how he woke Steven in the morning—tapped on the glass from the outside. "Okay, Moonshadow," Lily said. She went out and sat down on the balcony with him. As he walked back and forth in front of her, she pet his back. Each time she got to his hips, he arched his back high. She learned early on if she didn't join him out there, Moonshadow would claw the screen until he got his nails caught in it. Then, Lily had to unstick his claws, which never seemed very pleasant for him. With one arm stuck straight up and his other paw flat on the ground, it made for quite a stretch.

Lily sat out on the balcony with Moonshadow until he decided it was time to go back inside. Lily was grateful she and Steven had chosen a unit on that side of the building when they'd moved in. The other side of the building didn't have balconies, and they'd had no idea they'd wind up with a cute, little gray and white kitty whose outdoor time meant so much to him every day.

In the evening, Lily and Steven heard a strangled meow come from the bedroom. They panicked something might have happened to Moonshadow. He spent all afternoon in there in a patch of sunlight on the bed after coming back from the balcony. Lily and Steven rushed in to find Moonshadow staring down at a toy mouse. He set his paw upon the mouse, looked up at them, and once again, meowed loudly as if summoning a lion's fearful roar. Lily laughed. Steven grinned at Moonshadow's ferocity in the face of the toy mouse.

"He's teaching us how to hunt," Lily said. "He's trying to help. We're such stupid humans, we keep giving him cat food instead of fresh food."

In the night, while Lily and Steven were watching television, Moonshadow came out of their bedroom. With the cat sharing so much of their space with them, Lily took a handful of medications to manage her allergies, but it was worth it. When he entered the living room, Moonshadow meowed once. He looked at the two humans sitting on the couch, and he returned to the bedroom, looking over his shoulder at Lily and Steven the whole time. Lily and Steven followed Moonshadow. He nuzzled with them after they settled into bed as if he himself were tucking them in. Then, he ran a few errands of his own—food, water, litter box—and he climbed back up into the bed to fall asleep at Lily's feet and start the whole routine over again in the morning.

"It must have been very hard on Moonshadow to be homeless," Lily whispered as they settled into sleep. "He loves his simple pleasures, and he's such a creature of habit. He couldn't have had any of that out on the streets. I wish I'd found him earlier. I wish our little kitty hadn't had to live such a tough life. Maybe he wouldn't be so sick if somebody like me had given him a home when he was younger. I wish I could have known him when he was a kitten. I'm sure he was such a cute kitten with his little personality. You know, I can picture him back then. I wish I could have known him."

* * * *

Nearly two years after Lily first found him, one night while Steven was asleep and Lily was out of town, Moonshadow fell off the edge of the bed. Steven was startled awake by the noise. Moonshadow meowed from the floor. "Are you okay?" Steven asked the cat. Moonshadow meowed once more as if to say he was alright, and he climbed back up into bed with Steven.

The next morning, however, Moonshadow had a little scrape on his pink nose that Steven figured must have happened when he fell, and the cat was limping a bit. "Hurt yourself last night, huh, guy?" he asked Moonshadow. Steven smiled at the cat and scratched him under his chin. Moonshadow purred.

As Steven got ready for work, Moonshadow patrolled the perimeter of his and Lily's bed. Then, the usually sure-footed cat slipped, stumbled, and fell off the edge of the bed once again. One paw's nails got stuck in the comforter. With a piercing meow, Moonshadow cried out. Steven turned and looked. Moonshadow hung from a single paw off the edge of the bed. Steven rushed over and helped the cat untangle himself. He set Moonshadow gently onto the ground. "You need to be more careful," Steven said. "I won't be here all day to keep an eye on you."

When Lily got home that night, Steven recounted Moonshadow's adventures from the night before to her. As he told the story, he noticed Lily's face turning inward. "What's wrong?" Steven asked.

"Trouble maintaining balance is a sign of late-stage kidney disease," Lily said. She looked over at the cat lying on their bed. Even with his scraped-up nose, he appeared comfortable licking his paws on the extra blanket they kept at the foot of the bed for him to lie upon.

They didn't take Moonshadow to the vet right away. As long as Moonshadow wasn't in pain, they agreed there was nothing the vet could do other than confirm what they already knew—Moonshadow was dying. But then, one night as they slept, Moonshadow's piercing roar split the apartment. Unlike when he'd caught a toy mouse, however, this time, it didn't stop. They discovered the cat stumbling around the apartment and lying in different cool patches on the floor as if he were trying to, but couldn't, get comfortable. Steven and Lily took Moonshadow to the vet the following day.

The vet told them what they already knew, Moonshadow's kidney disease had grown worse. The vet stuck Moonshadow with a needle and filled him full with a bag of fluids. A watery bulge appeared on Moonshadow's back, which the vet said would slowly drain through the rest of his body. The vet took Moonshadow into the back to draw more blood and urine. When the cat came back, he looked tired and defeated. He tried running out of the room where Steven and Lily were waiting. When he couldn't get out the door, he searched every corner for an escape. He wailed a morose yowl. The vet taught Steven and Lily how to get the needle into Moonshadow's skin so the two of them could give the cat fluids at home. With the way Moonshadow was acting, they didn't want to have to bring the cat back to the vet every two weeks.

The next afternoon, the vet called Lily to give her the results from Moonshadow's blood work. There was an experimental steroid they could put Moonshadow on, the vet said. It was the same steroid Lance Armstrong had once used. It might help Moonshadow recover, but it might not make a difference. It was very expensive, and the vet told Lily they were in the realm of months of life for Moonshadow, not years. Lily told the vet to write the prescription, and when Steven got home, she discussed with him getting the steroid for Moonshadow. Steven agreed they should do it. Lily also told him they had to take Moonshadow back to the vet once again in two weeks to get more blood and urine drawn to ensure the drug was working. Neither of them felt very happy about that, but they agreed they needed to do it for Moonshadow's sake. Even though, the cat didn't understand English well enough to be told the suffering he would have to undergo would be for his own benefit.

When they brought Moonshadow back to the vet two weeks later, the cat started yowling as soon as they entered the door to the office. Once again, he tried running out of the room where they waited for the vet. He never hissed at or scratched anyone, but he never stopped looking for an escape route either. He appeared traumatized by his previous experience. Lily started crying when the vet took a horrified looking Moonshadow into the back once again to draw blood and urine.

After the visit, Steven and Lily decided they couldn't do that to Moonshadow again, not if the only difference were the possibility of just a few more months of life during which the cat would have to go through that experience with the vet every two weeks. Lily and Steven decided to take Moonshadow off the experimental steroid. They wanted to let him live out his last days in peace.

It took Lily and Steven a couple days to realize Moonshadow had gone blind. He'd had a hemorrhage in one of his eyes—another symptom of kidney failure—but, even with the shock of blood discoloring his iris, it still seemed he was able to see for a little while after that. One morning, however, when the cat bumped his head on an open drawer at the bottom of Lily's dresser, the two humans realized their little friend had been following the perimeter of the room, feeling the walls with his whiskers for nearly a week by then.

"I think it might be time," Steven said.

Lily held back tears. She nodded. She agreed. At their last visit to the vet, the vet had told them to keep an eye on what Moonshadow was still able to enjoy. As long as he still had pleasures in life, the vet had said, there was no need to take any further actions. By then, however, even Lily had to admit Moonshadow wasn't enjoying anything anymore. He didn't tap them in the morning. He never went out on the balcony anymore. It had been months since they'd last heard his ferocious roar. He no longer herded them into the bedroom when it was time to say goodnight. Lily hugged Moonshadow close. He'd grown so thin over the past weeks. His bones rubbed hard against her chest. She asked Steven if they could call a vet that would come to their apartment to put him to sleep. Even at the end of his life, she didn't want to take Moonshadow back to the vet in Tenleytown. He'd suffered too much already.

The vet came out on a Friday afternoon. Lily set Moonshadow on the bed in his favorite patch of sunlight. The vet gave Moonshadow an opiate to ease his pain. Then, she asked Steven and Lily if there was anything special they wanted to do for Moonshadow before he went to sleep one last time. Steven said he'd like to play them all a song. The sun shone brightly through the window. The vet gave Moonshadow one final injection as Cat Stevens sang over the radio.

And What Might Those Ideas Be?

Eric was driving back into the city after work. As usual, the traffic on the beltway was bumper to bumper. He passed the Mormon Temple across the beltway to his left. The giant structure looked like something out of *The Lord of the Rings*. It glimmered in the evening light, and it spoke of divine possibilities.

As he passed it, Eric imagined an army of orcs rushing down out of the mountains of Western Maryland where Eric was originally from. They stormed the castle and took it hostage. They painted its white walls red and refashioned the golden implements adorning it out of black ore. What was celestial was now infernal. What was sublime was now inferior.

Alone in his car, Eric smirked. He hadn't had a fantasy like that in years. It reminded him of his childhood and teenage years, when he'd ridden through the world in his parents' backseat with headphones wrapped over his ears. It must have had something to do with the music he was listening to right then, a recent recommendation from *Pitchfork* magazine that he'd saved to listen to on his way home from work that evening. Very cool. Very inspiring.

Eric thought back to when he'd been younger and he'd allowed his imagination to run off like that for hours on end. He wished he could do that again. But back then, the world had been so full of possibilities. Nowadays, everything seemed dead.

Then, pulling him from his reverie, right before he

reached Georgia Ave, the traffic came to an abrupt stop. Pushing his foot onto the brake, Eric slammed his hand hard against the steering wheel. "Come the fuck on," he shouted, but nobody was with him in the car to hear. The music continued to play. Eric glanced once again out the driver's side window to his left. But this time, instead of looking up, he looked down.

A leather-bound journal was pushed up against the Jersey barrier dividing the inner loop from the outer loop. A curious look spread across Eric's face. He didn't know why a journal would have been thrown out on the beltway. He chuckled a quiet laugh to himself. "What the fuck?" he said. But he started thinking...

Maybe some younger brother while they were on the way to visit their dad in PG County had grabbed his sister's diary out of her hands as she scribbled love letters to a non-existent boyfriend in its margins.

"Give that back!" she'd shouted in the backseat of their parents' car.

But before their mother could say anything to them about it, with a wicked grin, the younger brother had rolled down his window and thrown his sister's diary out into oncoming traffic. A silver Nissan Sentra had swerved to miss it, and then, in the backdraft, the journal had blown into the barrier.

Or maybe a University of Maryland student had been driving home. As he rounded a corner on the beltway, his throat closed up. Afraid his secret escapades would be revealed if his mother opened the journal he kept beside himself everywhere he went, he realized he needed to get rid of the book on the seat beside him immediately. In a burst of fear, while he was slowing down in traffic as he approached Georgia Ave, he threw his journal out the window. Even if it ever were to be found, nobody would know who had written those secret thoughts, desires, and experiences. Nobody would ever know he was the one who'd slept with his RA on a night when nobody was looking.

Or maybe it was the journal of a writer or an artist from Columbia Heights. It had been put on top of a box to keep safe while the artist was moving out to Takoma Park. But while the box sat on a pickup truck's bed, wind ripped open the tape, and the journal flew out. It landed on the beltway. The artist never even realized it was gone until he showed up at his new home. He tore through all his boxes, certain he'd packed it, before collapsing in a heap of tears at all the lost ideas.

And what might those ideas be?

They could have been a series of sketches for a magnificent painting of Malcolm X Park. Without the sketches, the painting would never get done. The commission would never be completed. The artist might have to start over from scratch—one line here, another line there. Until eventually, the piece was somehow recreated from memory. But the artist could never be certain the finished product was the same as he'd originally envisioned. No line can ever be drawn the exact same way twice. No moment can ever be recreated perfectly again.

Or the notebook could have been filled with chord changes and lyrics for a non-existent album. The musician might remember some of her words from shows she'd played at the Black Cat, but muscle memory would never recreate every shape of her chords. She'd struggle on her guitar. Trying to remember how this note fed into that one, she'd bend her fingers every which way. But it was no use. Without the journal, she'd never remember the album she'd created.

Or it could have been filled with a collection of short

stories about Washington, DC. The pages might have covered all the intricacies of the city Eric lived in. It's passion. It's hardship. It's beauty. It's identity. The author would now have to recollect those stories from memory. He'd have to recall every idea he'd had and rewrite the ones he could remember. With the tip of a pen dangling from the corner of his mouth, he'd have to sit in front of a different open notebook. He'd have to wrack his brain, but he'd never be able to remember everything. The ideas in their infancy were gone.

But that notebook might still inspire Eric to create something of his own. The words he read in it might spark some idea that would turn into his own great novel. Creation breeds creation, and one person's unfinished work could turn into another person's masterpiece. Eric always knew he had a book hidden inside himself somewhere. He simply needed something to fulfill him, something to bring it out.

Eric might even be able to read the poems in that notebook to his friends when they stopped by his apartment in Petworth. Together, he and his friends would analyze the meter and cadence of the unknown poet. They'd discuss the merits of the great work Eric had discovered. The author might never be found, but Eric's friends would encourage him to publish it anonymously anyway. Then, one day, the unknown author would appear at the publishers to claim her royalty checks. She'd be inducted into the glittering literati, and Eric would be lauded as the discoverer of a great talent, a great movement.

Or maybe Eric could pass off the writing in the notebook as his own. He could use it to seduce women he brought home from the bars on 11th Street. They'd find his insights brilliant, and they'd never know the words Eric shared with them weren't his own. Until one night, the notebook's true author would show up at Eric's place as the friend of a friend who Eric had invited over.

Eric would read the words aloud, and the author would shout, "Hey, man! I wrote that. Who the fuck do you think you are? Give me back my notebook!" Everybody in Eric's apartment would stare at him, and Eric would have to admit the truth. The girlfriend he'd seduced with those words would leave him. Eric would be left alone.

Eric glanced up. He looked in his rearview mirror. The person in the car behind him was looking forward. She wasn't glancing over at the notebook against the Jersey barrier. She had no idea it was there. She had no idea what it might contain. The notebook was Eric's secret. The woman behind him might hit her horn if Eric opened his door and jumped out, but she wouldn't be able to do anything about it.

Eric glanced to his right. The cars beside him were stuck in traffic as well. The entire beltway had come to a standstill. If Eric wanted, he could easily leave his car, retrieve the notebook, and see what it was all about, whether it was the property of a teenage girl or a local musician, whether it was full of secret musings or great literature.

But there might be a cop somewhere in that lineup of cars as well. The cop might see Eric get out of his car, and when he saw that, he might hit his lights. The cars would part like the Red Sea. The cop would drive straight up to Eric, and Eric would have to admit he was stealing somebody else's life. But the cop wouldn't care about that. He'd simply give Eric a ticket for getting out of his car on the beltway.

Suddenly, Eric saw himself ripping off his seatbelt. He whipped open his door, leaped onto the beltway, ran to the Jersey barrier, and grabbed that notebook. He'd discover what was in it. He needed to know the truth about the person who had owned it before him, the person from whose hands it had slipped onto the open road. Eric needed to know what that notebook said.

With greedy fingers, Eric returned to his car. He sat down before the traffic started moving again, and he opened the notebook.

But it was empty. Nobody had ever even had a chance to write their name in it. Eric sat still in his car. In disbelief, he flipped through the empty pages. The woman behind him laid into her horn. The traffic was starting up again. But Eric couldn't move. He was staring at the notebook's empty pages. He was crying. At least, that's what Eric imagined.

Instead, as the album he'd read about on *Pitchfork* earlier that day continued to play, Eric sat still in his car on the beltway daydreaming. The traffic wasn't going anywhere. The world is so full of possibilities.

Thank You

This collection of stories started as a simple observation. When traveling outside of Washington, DC, the city I lived in back in 2014, I realized most Americans didn't think of my adopted home as a real place. It was a gathering point for politicians and media execs, a "swamp" of power and intrigue. Living in the city, however, I found it to be full of people dealing with their own personal hopes and frustrations, some of whom happened to work in politics or the media, but all of whom were no different from the people I met outside the city. So I'd like to start with a very special thank you to the citizens of that home of mine from 2005-2007 and again from 2012-2018: Washington, DC. None of these stories could have come to be without your experiences and dreams.

I'd also like to thank the members of my DC writing group with whom I met on a regular basis throughout the composition of these 14 stories: Adam Brown, Gareth Frank, E.J. Wenstrom, Chris Peot, and Andrew McGuire. Without your reading and assistance, these stories never would have come to be what they are today. Thank you for taking the time to read, edit, and comment on them.

And finally I'd like to thank all my family and friends, but especially my wife, PJ Adams, for all of her support, encouragement, and constructive criticism as I wrote these stories. I love you.

Portrait by PJ Adams

About the Author

*M*ichael Anthony Adams, Jr. is originally from Whittier, CA. He holds a master's degree in Philosophy from the New School for Social Research in New York City. As a teenager, he was the lead vocalist for Richmond, VA-based hardcore band Broken Chains of Segregation. He's the founder of Ursprung Collective, a spoken word/music project referred to as "fantastic brain food" on ReverbNation. He was the primary lyricist on indie rock group One & the Many's first two albums, *Forms* and *Hours*. His writing has appeared in the *Santa Fe Literary Review*, *The Stray Branch*, *Badlands Literary Journal*, and more. He currently lives with his wife, PJ Adams, and their children in Baltimore, MD.

www.MichaelAnthonyAdamsJr.com

Printed in the USA
CPSIA information can be obtained
at www.ICGtesting.com
LVHW040250210624
783561LV00008B/975